D0378993

Ra the Mighty

THE CROCODILE CAPER

Ra
the
Mighty

THE CROCODILE
CAPER

BY
A. B. Greenfield

ILLUSTRATED BY
Sarah Horne

HOLIDAY HOUSE · New York

Text copyright © 2020 by Amy Butler Greenfield
Illustrations copyright © 2020 by Sarah Horne
All Rights Reserved
HOLIDAY HOUSE is registered in the U.S. Patent and Trademark Office.
Printed and bound in September 2020 at Maple Press, York, PA, USA.
The artwork was created with pen and ink with a digital finish.
www.holidayhouse.com
First Edition
1 3 5 7 9 10 8 6 4 2

Library of Congress Cataloging-in-Publication Data
Names: Greenfield, Amy Butler, 1968- author. | Horne, Sarah, 1979–
illustrator.
Title: Ra the mighty : the crocodile caper / by A. B. Greenfield ;
illustrated by Sarah Horne.
Other titles: Crocodile caper
Description: First edition. | New York : Holiday House, [2020] | Includes
bibliographical references. | Audience: Ages 7–10. | Audience: Grades
2–3. | Summary: Ra, the pharoah's pampered cat, and his scarab beetle
sidekick, Khepri, investigate when crown prince Dedi disappears from the
palace of one of Pharoah's wives in ancient Egypt.
Identifiers: LCCN 2019055118 | ISBN 9780823446490 (hardcover)
Subjects: CYAC: Cats—Fiction. | Scarabs—Fiction. | Missing
children—Fiction. | Smuggling—Fiction. | Egypt—History—To 332
B.C.—Fiction. | Mystery and detective stories.
Classification: LCC PZ7.G8445 Rc 2020 | DDC [Fic]—dc23
LC record available at https://lccn.loc.gov/2019055118

ISBN: 978-0-8234-4649-0 (hardcover)
ISBN: 978-0-8234-4999-6 (paperback)

For Milo and Gideon,
mighty readers and brothers
—A.B.G.

CHAPTER 1

A Nile Cruise

I am Ra the Mighty, Pharaoh's Cat, Lord of the Powerful Paw. Everyone knows I'm special. That's why they bring me offerings. And by offerings, I mean snacks—the best in all of Egypt.

"I can't wait." I pranced onto the royal barge. It was anchored at the palace docks, ready for my voyage down the Nile with Pharaoh. "I hear they've stewed an oxtail just for me."

"Oxtail? Seriously?" said a tiny voice between my ears. It came from my best buddy, Khepri. He's a scarab beetle, and he likes to perch there. "I don't know how you can eat that stuff. Give me dung balls any day."

I sighed. Like most scarab beetles, Khepri lives for dung. (Disgusting, I know. Don't think I haven't told him.) "Keep it to yourself, buddy."

"I hope they have some ox dung for me," he murmured. "Though I'll settle for horse."

"Khepri, please!" I stretched out in a sunny spot on the deck. "You're spoiling my appetite."

"Is that even possible?" a mild voice asked. Turning my head, I saw my friend Miu, the kitchen cat. She was gliding out of the cook's quarters.

"Miu, did they bring my oxtail on board?" I asked.

"And is there any ox dung?" Khepri chirped.

"I have no idea," Miu said briskly as sailors tramped past us. "But there's something going on, you two. A change in plans. I heard the cook grumbling, but he didn't say much. We should find out what's happening."

"Ra, did you hear that?" Khepri leaped down to the gleaming deck. "It's a mystery!"

"Make it go away." I rolled over, narrowly

avoiding more sailors. "I mean, I know we're Great Detectives—"

"The Greatest," Khepri put in modestly.

"—but we've already solved two mysteries, and I think that's enough for anyone." I closed my eyes to block the sun's glare. "Anyway, this is supposed to be a pleasure cruise. The next few days are for snacking and sleeping."

"I wouldn't bet on it," Miu said. "I saw Kiya headed this way."

"What?!" I flipped over in shock. "Pharaoh said she was going in the other boat—"

"I think she wants to visit you before we sail," Miu told me.

"I'm getting off!" I shrieked. I darted forward, then froze. Kiya was coming on board with scraps of linen in her hands.

"Don't be silly, Ra," Miu scolded me. "She's Pharaoh's daughter. She's part of your family. And she's only six years old. What is there to be so scared of?"

"You don't understand, Miu," I yowled in despair. *"It's dress-up time!"*

Pounce! Kiya grabbed me around the belly and scooped me up.

3

"Hi, Ra-baby!" she cooed.

Ra-baby. Of all the silly, goopy names . . .

"It's Ra the Mighty," I meowed. "Lord of the Powerful Paw."

But she didn't understand me. No surprises there. Humans never do, even the small ones.

"Come on, Ra-baby." She lugged me over to the shade in front of Pharaoh's decktop cabin, built to protect him from the relentless sun. "I've found you some great new clothes."

Let me set the record straight, in case you're like Kiya and you have some funny ideas about felines. *Cats don't wear clothes.*

Okay, okay. They wear a little jewelry sometimes. I admit I'm quite attached to the bead necklace Pharaoh gave me when I was a kitten. But clothes?

Never.

Ever.

Try telling that to Kiya, though. "Ra-baby, how about we put on your head scarf first?"

Head scarf?

 4

"You're going to look so cute with your ears tucked under it!" Kiya chortled.

"Did you hear that?" I yowled to Khepri and Miu. "Get me out of here!"

I squirmed and clawed at the linen.

"Ra, be careful!" Miu warned me. "You don't want to hurt her. Remember, you're one of Bastet's own, sworn to protect children. Especially the children of your very own family."

With her torn ear and grizzled coat, Miu looks like a tough customer, but her heart's as soft as they come. And she was right. I'm one of Bastet's own. All cats are, but me more than most, since I'm one of the great cat goddess's direct descendants.

Still, it took me a moment to remember my royal duty and retract my claws.

"Silly Ra-baby." Kiya smooched me. "Now let's put on your veil."

No claws, I told myself. *No claws, no teeth, no claws, no teeth—*

"KIYA!" a voice boomed. A voice that made me pull my claws in as far as they could go. A voice that made Kiya jump.

I twisted my head back, and there he was,

standing on the deck: the Ruler of Rulers, the Lord of the Two Lands, the High Priest of Every Temple.

Also known as Pharaoh, Kiya's father.

He was my human. And the moment I saw him, I knew something was wrong.

CHAPTER 2

Ra-baby

"Kiya, what are you doing to poor Ra?" Pharaoh demanded.

"I'm dressing him up, Daddy!" Kiya held me so her father could see.

"Well, I don't think he likes it, Kiya."

"Sure he does, Daddy. He's my Ra-baby."

I twisted in her hands and bolted down the deck, leaving the head scarf behind. She gathered the linens and started to stalk me. "Here, Ra-baby! Come and play!"

No way. I leaped onto the roof of Pharaoh's royal cabin.

"Leave Ra alone, Kiya, and come here. I have news for you." Pharaoh motioned to a tall boy behind him. "And for Dedi, too."

Maybe you've heard of Ramses Dedumose, Pharaoh's oldest son and heir? We call him Dedi, and he's the Great Son, the crown prince. Not that he looked too princely that morning. He was just a twelve-year-old boy with long, skinny legs and a thoughtful expression in his eyes. Still, I was fond of him. He had a real talent for mischief, like his sister, but fortunately he had a smidgen more sense. For one thing, he had never tried to dress me up.

Kiya skipped over to Pharaoh. "What is it, Daddy?"

"I have to stay here in Thebes for a few more days," Pharaoh said. "Something has come up."

"Daddy, no!" Kiya cried. Dedi looked disappointed. But not as disappointed as I was. *What about my oxtail?*

"Never mind," Pharaoh told his children. "There's no reason why you two shouldn't sail today. The festival is over, and your royal mother will be longing to see you."

Well, that would put plenty of distance between me and Kiya. I stifled a yowl of delight.

Pharaoh added gravely, "Besides, Thebes isn't the best place for you to be right now, under the circumstances."

I couldn't agree more: Thebes was definitely not a good place for Kiya to be. Not while I was in it, anyway.

"What circumstances?" Dedi asked. "What's going on?"

"Nothing for you to worry about," Pharaoh said. "The point is that you will set out today. Lady Satiah has invited you to spend the night at her palace on the Nile."

"Lady Satiah?" Dedi wrinkled his nose.

I wrinkled my nose, too. Despite her beauty, Lady Satiah isn't the kind of person who warms anyone's heart, including mine. I don't think she even warms Pharaoh's heart, although she's one of his wives. His father set up the marriage as a favor to one of Egypt's most powerful lords. Like most political matches, it didn't work out. Pharaoh and Lady Satiah haven't lived together for years.

After Lady Satiah had her royal son, Ahmose, she went to live in one of the more remote palaces. The Great Wife insisted on that. As everyone in Egypt knows, the Great Wife is Pharaoh's *real* wife: the partner of his heart and the mother of almost all of his children, including Dedi and Kiya. (Plus she's fond of cats—especially me.)

"We can't stay with Lady Satiah!" Kiya cried. "She hates us."

"Don't be ridiculous," Pharaoh said patiently. "Lady Satiah does not hate you."

"Yes, she does," Kiya insisted. "She's awful."

Pharaoh frowned—a sight that made even Kiya go quiet. "Lady Satiah is a noble and gracious lady. If she was strict with you two last year, it was because you deserved it. Have you forgotten that you stuck a lizard in her bed?"

Kiya and Dedi exchanged a joyous look.

"Oh, we remember," Dedi said.

"We did it because she was so horrible," Kiya explained. "She was horrible first. She—"

"I don't want to hear any more," Pharaoh said, his voice a low rumble of thunder. "Lady Satiah is one of my wives, and she deserves your respect. That is final. Understood?"

Dedi bowed his head. "Yes, Dad."

Kiya pouted at first, but when Pharaoh's frown deepened she gave in. "Yes, Daddy."

"Very good." Pharaoh put his arms around them both. "Judging from her letter, she is eager to see you. If you mind your manners, all will be well."

"Can't you come with us?" Kiya pleaded.

"I wish I could," Pharaoh told her. "But never fear, you'll have plenty of company."

I listened with half an ear as he explained who was going: Kiya's nursemaid, four of Pharaoh's guards, and a whole boatload of sailors. They were also taking a cook, but that didn't bother me. Pharaoh has dozens of cooks, so there would be plenty of them left to make my snacks here in Thebes while I waited for Pharaoh to finish his business.

"You will also travel with Ra the Mighty," Pharaoh told the children. "He is a favorite of the gods, and he will keep you safe."

What?! My ears swiveled, and I lost my balance. I fell from the cabin roof.

Pharaoh, Dedi, and Kiya turned around as I landed feetfirst.

"Silly Ra-baby," Kiya said fondly, coming up to me. "Isn't it great that you're coming with us? We can play dress-up all day!"

"Noooooooooooooooooo!" I yowled.

"Ah!" Pharaoh said, looking pleased. "That's the sound he makes when he's warding off intruders. He's trying to protect you already." Bending down to rub the fur between my ears, he added, "I know I can trust you, Ra. Do what you must to keep my children from harm."

Never let it be said that Pharaoh's Cat doesn't know his duty. If Pharaoh was ordering me to protect his children, then protect them I would. But as Kiya grinned down at me, I only had one thought:

Who was going to protect *me*?

CHAPTER 3

Danger, Ahoy!

Have you ever cruised down the Nile? If not, I'll let you in on a secret—a royal barge is the way to go. Pharaoh has several at his disposal. Built of pricy cedar from Lebanon, they're fitted out with top-grade quarters for the family (and for Pharaoh's Cat).

We set off at noon, and I claimed my usual nook near the bow, where I could enjoy the cool river breezes.

"Wow," Khepri said from the top of my head. "Look at that view!"

As we slipped away from Thebes, the great temple shone like polished ivory in the noonday sun. A light breeze made the water sparkle like jewels. Perfect napping conditions!

Miu trotted over to me. "Dedi is talking with the captain, but I think you'd better keep an eye on Kiya, Ra. She's checking out every inch of this ship. The sailors aren't happy about it."

"Oh, let her explore," I said airily. "If the sailors are unhappy, that's their problem."

Miu wasn't looking too happy herself. "But—"

"Look!" I meowed in delight. "Here come the snacks!"

Sure enough, the cook was headed our way. He set a platter in front of me and headed back to the kitchen.

"Oxtail!" I licked my chops in approval. "Miu, there's some for you, too."

"There's no dung," Khepri said sadly.

"I smelled something stinky on a sailor's sandals," Miu told him.

Khepri brightened. "Thanks!" He scuttled off happily.

Normally, snack time is my favorite time of the day. I love that it comes around so often. But as I chomped on my oxtail, Kiya crept past a knot of sailors so she could watch me. It made me nervous.

After I lapped up the last trace of sauce, I said to Miu, "You know what? It's been a long day already, and I could use a nap. I think I'll go lie down for a while."

"No napping, Ra," Miu said sternly. "You've got to look after the children. Kiya especially."

"I thought maybe you could do that, Miu. You're so good with kids."

Miu didn't budge. "Ra, these are Pharaoh's kids, and you're Pharaoh's Cat. It's your duty to look after them."

"But think how nice you'd look in a head scarf," I pleaded.

I was still pleading when Kiya pounced. "Ra-baby! Time to play dress-up! Here we go." She whipped out a piece of linen and tugged it over my head. "That's your tunic. Now let's wrap you up."

I was too startled to meow, but I heard a tiny giggle and looked up. Khepri was watching, with Miu right behind him, a tiny cat grin on her face.

"You look quite fetching, Ra," she purred.

"Actually, he looks like a mummy," Khepri said. "Only with more fur."

I looked down. I *did* look like a mummy. I twisted, trying to free myself. And when Kiya draped me in yet more linen, I showed my teeth.

"Ra!" Miu sounded shocked. "Calm down. She's being quite gentle, for a six-year-old. And it's not the end of the world to play dress-up."

"It isn't for us, anyway," Khepri put in. "It's fun to watch."

Miu gave him a cat wink. "So it is."

"Sweet Ra-baby." Kiya smooched the top of my head. "Now be a good kitty and let me put on your loincloth."

A *loincloth*?

"Okay. That's it. I'm done!" With a thrust of my powerful paws, I broke free. Darting past Dedi, who was striding toward Kiya, I climbed straight up the mast, shedding linen as I went.

"Ra-baby, come back!" Kiya wailed.

"Never!" I cried.

"You don't have to be a pharaoh, Ra-baby." Kiya waggled a tiny veil in the breeze. "You can be a high priestess instead."

I didn't dignify that with a response.

"I'll give you seconds of stewed oxtail," Kiya wheedled. "And all my snacks."

I was tempted, but only for a second. There are some sacrifices I'm not prepared to make, not even for snacks.

"I'm coming after you!" Kiya lunged for the mast.

I scrambled up a little higher, but there was no need. Dedi pried his sister away. "Kiya, stop it. If you want to be friends with Ra, that's not the way. Leave him alone for a while, and come and play Twenty Squares with me."

Kiya pouted, but the promise of a board game with her brother won her over. After that, I lost track of time. For hours, I hung out on the mast, curled tight against a rolled-up sail. I heard fishermen shouting as they paddled out of our way, and flocks of geese honking as they rose from the reedy shore. But mostly it was quiet. Lulled by the bobbing of the ship, I lounged in blissful, uninterrupted peace.

After a long while, I heard a familiar click by my ear.

"I can't believe you're up here." Khepri

clambered onto the mast, breathless from climbing so high. "You're supposed to be guarding Pharaoh's kids."

"I can guard them from here," I told him. "In fact, this is the perfect place to do it. Up here, I can see everything."

It was true. From my lofty perch, I could look down at Kiya and Dedi and the entire barge. And my view didn't end there. Gazing out to the horizon, I could see the Nile coiling through the desert like a long, swollen snake. Thanks to Pharaoh's expertly performed rites, the gods had blessed Egypt with the best floods in living memory. The river was growing wider almost by the hour.

"See the small figure down on the front deck?" I said to Khepri. "The one bouncing up and down? That's Kiya, bugging her brother—"

"Why do people say *bug* when they mean *annoy*?" Khepri wanted to know. "Bugs are nice!"

"It's just an expression," I said.

"It's not a very good one," he said as he climbed onto my paw.

"Khepri, my point is that if you look down, you'll see—"

"I can't." Khepri closed his eyes and nestled closer to me.

"What do you mean, you can't?"

"I'm scared of heights," Khepri admitted. "Especially on boats. I get seasick."

"Then what are you doing up here?" I asked.

"I was worried about you."

You know, bugs actually *are* nice. Khepri is, anyway. "I'm fine," I told him. "But thanks for the concern, my friend. Want to hop on my back?"

"Er . . . you won't make any sudden moves, will you?"

"I'll be steady as a rock," I promised.

After Khepri got himself settled, he added, "I'm also worried about what kept Pharaoh in Thebes. He just said *something has come up.*"

"Oh, stuff is always coming up for Pharaoh." I yawned. "Some priest probably wants to drone on about next year's festival plans. Or maybe a vizier has another dull report to make. People are always boring the sandals off Pharaoh." Not for the first time, I thought how much better it was to be Pharaoh's Cat.

"It's strange that he didn't say what was wrong," Khepri persisted.

"Who says anything's wrong?"

"Don't you remember? Pharaoh said he didn't think Thebes was the best place for the children to be right now."

"Probably because they would interrupt him," I said.

"Or maybe he thought Thebes wasn't safe," Khepri suggested. "He seemed awfully worried about them not coming to harm."

I felt a twitch of uneasiness but refused to give in to it. "You're letting your imagination run away with you."

"But Great Detectives need imagination," Khepri argued. "It's how we solve mysteries. Like this one."

"There is no mystery," I told him. "Pharaoh is fine. If anyone's in danger today, it's me—from Kiya." I turned my head into the wind and added happily, "Though not while I'm up here."

"You won't be for much longer," Khepri said. "Miu said to warn you we'll be arriving at Lady Satiah's soon."

"Why didn't Miu come up here to tell me herself?" I asked. "She's not afraid of heights." Miu isn't afraid of much.

"She says somebody has to look after the children." Khepri paused. "To be honest, Ra, she's not too pleased with you right now. You left Kiya and Dedi to fend for themselves."

"I'm still guarding them," I huffed. "Just... from a distance."

"A really long distance," Khepri said.

There are plenty of servants around to look after them," I pointed out. "And anyway, Miu ought to understand that everyone needs some time to unwind. Especially me. It's not like I'm cut out for this role. I'm Ra the Mighty, Pharaoh's Cat, Lord of the Powerful Paw. I'm not Ra the Mighty, Royal Babysitter."

"It was funny watching Kiya dress you up." On my back, Khepri giggled. "I loved the mummy look."

"It's not so great from the inside," I told him.

Below us, at the captain's command, the crew bent to their oars. I looked downriver. Green shores hugged the river close, then yielded to the vast, bleached sands of the desert, glowing in the late afternoon sun. At the next bend in the river, you could see the palace, so close to the Nile that it seemed to be floating. Behind high walls and a moat, its smooth, whitewashed buildings gleamed like pearls.

Connected to the palace by a bridge, an immense stone landing jutted out into the Nile, with piers extending from it like teeth. Boats of all sizes were tied up and anchored there.

"I guess that's where we're meant to dock," Khepri said. "But why are there so many loose logs in the water?"

"Maybe a pier fell apart in the floodwaters," I said.

"Meeeeeeeoooooooooooooooow!" Miu was climbing toward us, a head scarf tied around her neck. "Ra! Khepri! Where are you? We're almost at the palace docks, and there are crocodiles *everywhere*."

Alarmed, I took another look at those logs

floating near the palace. Now that we were closer, I could see they had scaly skin. And tails. And teeth.

"Crocodiles!" Khepri gulped. "Dozens and dozens of them!"

"Now, don't get worried," I told him. "Crocodiles may look fierce, but they're animals just like us."

"Only with more teeth," Khepri said.

"Er . . . yes. I wonder if those rumors about their blood sacrifices are true?"

"Blood sacrifices?" Khepri said in a tiny voice.

"Nobody knows the details because nobody wants to ask. But you know what they call their god Sobek, don't you? *Pointed of Teeth.*"

"Ra, this isn't making me feel better," Khepri said.

"I told you, there's no need to worry," I reassured him. "This is as close as you'll ever get to them. Once we're inside the palace, they can't touch us."

"You two need to come down," Miu called up to us. "I can't look after both children at once, and if Kiya falls in—"

Yikes! What would Pharaoh say if Kiya became crocodile food?

"We're coming!" I shouted. "Hang on tight, Khepri."

Pharaoh's Cat is an ace at climbing things, but getting down? Well, that's trickier, even for a cat with powerful paws. Going straight down the mast didn't appeal to me, so I used the ropes instead. I was nearly back on deck when my forepaw skidded forward.

"Watch your step!" Miu called up to me.

I was about to tell her that Pharaoh's Cat doesn't need to watch his step—he's naturally graceful—when my other forepaw slipped. My head went swinging over the water, with Khepri clinging to my ear.

A rumple-backed crocodile leaped for us, rising almost straight out of the river.

"Noooooooooooo!" Khepri and I shrieked.

How could a reptile jump so high? Its mouth snapped open, revealing a full set of white choppers.

Pointed of Teeth, I thought dizzily.

It was crocodile snack time. And we were on the menu.

CHAPTER 4

Crocodile Smile

Have I mentioned how much I like Dedi? That boy really takes after Pharaoh. Hearing my shriek, he ran to the railing and caught me. Khepri was holding on to me, of course, and we both landed safely on the deck.

Not that we had much time to catch our breath. A moment later, Kiya leaned over the side of the barge, "to see the crocodiles up close." Dedi hauled her back by her tunic, and they started tussling. Miu and I had to keep them from falling overboard.

"Where's Kiya's nursemaid?" I asked Miu. "She ought to be helping out here."

"She's got a sore foot, poor thing. So it's up to us to look after these children." Miu gave me a stern look. "That means no more shirking, Ra."

"Who's shirking?" I said. And it was the truth—at least for the next half hour. We herded Dedi and Kiya around the barge until it was time to disembark. Then we had a heart-stopping minute as they crossed the gangplank. Below us, the crocodiles gnashed their teeth.

By the time we finally entered the palace's spiked gates, the sun was dipping low over the flooded river. It was a relief to reach safety and proceed to the great hall. Though smaller than I was used to, the chamber was spectacular. Huge columns painted with lotus blossoms rose up from a floor as blue as the Nile.

"Thank goodness we're off that boat," Miu said as the children went forward, their footsteps echoing on the tiles. "We're out of danger now."

"I'm not so sure about that," Khepri said from his spot between my ears.

One glance ahead and I saw what he meant. At the far end of the hall, Lady Satiah sat on a thronelike golden chair, ready to receive us. Under an impressive wig, her bloodred lips were pressed tight together, without a hint of a welcoming smile. As the children came closer, her kohl-rimmed eyes narrowed, like a crocodile sighting prey.

My fur prickled. Out of danger? Not on your life. We were headed dead straight into it. Every instinct told me so.

"Dedi!" I meowed. "Kiya! Don't go any closer!" Determined to protect them, I hurtled forward, Miu at my heels.

Ahead of us, Kiya and Dedi stopped short, staring at something in Lady Satiah's lap.

From high on my head, Khepri whispered, "Is that a *crocodile*?"

"Yes," I said, stunned. "I think it is."

"A small one," Miu said after a moment.

"He doesn't look that small to me," Khepri murmured.

"And even small ones have teeth," I pointed out.

To be honest, I hadn't expected to see any kind of animal in Lady Satiah's lap. From what I could recall, she wasn't even fond of cats or dogs. So what was she doing with a crocodile?

Judging from her expression, maybe she was planning to turn it loose on Kiya and Dedi. If she did, would anyone stop her? Er . . . besides me, that is?

I glanced at the people next to Lady Satiah.

Standing closest to her was a man in his prime, dressed with military precision. He might be strong enough to take on a small crocodile, but he had a face as stolid as a tomb statue, and he didn't look like he was about to intervene.

Next to him was a much older man whose skin was almost as crinkled as the crocodile's. He was watching the crocodile closely, but he was dressed like a servant, and I doubted he would dare cross his mistress.

Standing awkwardly to one side was a bashful boy who kept looking anxiously at Lady Satiah. I recognized him as her son, Ahmose.

Lady Satiah stared balefully at Kiya and Dedi. "What do you two mean by sailing here alone?" she hissed. "Where is your father?"

"D-Daddy?" Faced with Lady Satiah's

anger, and her crocodile, even Kiya faltered. "He's . . . he's back in Thebes."

"He's very sorry he couldn't come," offered Dedi, who had been trained in diplomacy. "Perhaps he will visit later."

"Later, later," Lady Satiah repeated mockingly. "With him, it's always later. And his later means *never*."

"He is very busy—" Dedi began.

"I sent him a special invitation, and instead he sent you," Lady Satiah interrupted. "What am I supposed to do?"

"If you don't wish us to stay, we won't," Dedi said with dignity.

It was a brave answer, but also a foolish one. Where else could we stay? It's risky to navigate the Nile by night because there are so many sandbars. You need a navigator who knows the local currents, and we didn't have one. The only other place we could stay was the boat itself. I couldn't imagine trying to keep the crocodiles at bay . . .

"Very well," Lady Satiah snapped. "You can—"

The grim-faced man bent down and

whispered in her ear. He spoke so low that I couldn't hear every word, but he called her "sister" and said something about "our advantage."

Lady Satiah looked angry at first, then thoughtful. When her brother finished whispering, she gave Dedi a toothy smile.

"My dear Ramses Dedumose, don't be ridiculous. I am always delighted to have Pharaoh's honored children as my guests. And Ahmose is, too, aren't you, my love?" She turned to the shy boy. "After all, they are your brother and sister."

Ahmose nodded, but he wouldn't meet anyone's eyes.

Lady Satiah's lips tightened again, but she spoke with forced good cheer. "We have prepared a great feast, and you must dine with us. Perhaps we will think of a way to entice your dear father to visit very soon." Rising from her chair, she thrust the baby crocodile at the wrinkled servant. "Keeper of the Zoo, take this thing back to its cage."

The crocodile flew like a scaly package between them.

"Oh, do take care, my lady," the Keeper

murmured, nestling the crocodile in his arms. "They are delicate creatures, and he's only a baby."

Lady Satiah ignored him.

"A baby?" Miu's voice grew tender. "So that's why he's so small. The poor thing! What's he doing out here on his own?"

"They've tied his mouth shut," Khepri observed.

It was true. Now that the crocodile was closer, I could see the string. I guess it should have made me feel safer, but what I felt was indignant. Who wants to see a baby treated like that? Even if it is a baby crocodile.

At least he seemed to be in better hands now. The Keeper of the Zoo had a kindly face, and he cradled the crocodile in gentle hands.

"Don't worry, little one," the Keeper said soothingly. "There's a lovely supper waiting for you in the zoo. I'll bring you back there and untie those nasty knots."

As he ambled off with the crocodile, Khepri whispered, "She has a zoo? Nobody mentioned that before."

"I didn't know she had one," I said. "But I guess it's not so surprising. Zoos have become very fashionable. Every jumped-up son of a vizier wants one."

"I don't get it," Miu said. "What's so fun about seeing animals in cages?"

"Humans are strange," I agreed. "I think it's a way of showing off how much money they have. That kind of thing impresses other humans."

"They trap baby animals just so they can show off?" Miu was outraged. "That's dreadful. They should follow Pharaoh's example. He doesn't have one."

"He doesn't need a zoo," I said. "He has me."

"And luckily he's not fond of cages," Khepri added.

We were not the only ones interested in the crocodile. Kiya was watching the Keeper carry him off. She turned to Ahmose. "Can we go with them?"

"Sure." With an eager smile, Ahmose glanced from her to Dedi. "Both of you can come. I'll give you a tour—"

"Ahmose, where do you think you're

going?" Lady Satiah blocked the route forward.

Ahmose didn't even try to argue, but Kiya did. "We're going to the zoo!"

"The zoo is off-limits," Lady Satiah said sharply. "And we are about to dine. You may refresh yourselves before we gather in the banqueting room. Ahmose, show them the way."

Looking miserable, Ahmose shuffled off. Kiya and Dedi trailed behind him.

Lady Satiah turned to the grim-faced man and fixed him with a long stare. "Well, brother, this should be a night to remember." Her lips quirked.

"She's smiling like a crocodile," Khepri whispered as Lady Satiah and her brother left the hall. "I think she's up to something."

"Something bad," Miu agreed. "We'd better follow her."

We'd hardly taken more than a few paces, however, when a bird swooped down from the ceiling and dive-bombed us.

"Intruders!" he screamed. "Hit the decks! Oop-oop! You're under arrest!"

CHAPTER 5

Oop-Oop!

Before we could take cover, the bird screeched to a halt, landing on the back of Lady Satiah's empty gilded chair.

"Impressive, huh?" Flicking back his top-knot of multicolored feathers, he beamed down at us. "Did I scare you? Oop-oop! I bet I did."

As the bird puffed up his peach-colored chest, Khepri yipped in distress. "It's a hoopoe bird!" Scrambling off my head, he slid down to my belly fur.

"Hey, watch out," the hoopoe told me. "Your snack is getting away."

"He's not my snack," I said indignantly. "He's my buddy."

"Sorry! My mistake." The hoopoe fluttered

his topknot at me. "Oop-oop! Or maybe yours. They're good eating, dung beetles. I love that stinky smell when you crack them open."

Khepri whimpered and dug himself deeper into my belly fur. It tickled a bit, but I didn't blame him. I lowered my middle toward the floor, the better to hide him.

"Well, this beetle is off the menu," I told the hoopoe. "His name is Khepri, and he's under royal protection."

"Royal, huh?" The hoopoe looked us over. "Like the Lady Satiah?"

"Like Pharaoh," I said. "I'm Pharaoh's Cat."

The bird goggled at me. "Oop-oop! Guess I can't arrest you then!"

"You certainly can't," Miu told him. "In fact, who gave you the right to arrest anyone? You're just a hoopoe."

The hoopoe looked annoyed. "Is she with you, too?" he asked me.

"Yes," I said. "And if you want to keep Pharaoh happy, you'll show us around."

"That is, if you know where you're going," Miu put in.

"Know where I'm going? Oop-oop!" The hoopoe cackled at Miu. "Sister, I was born in the walls here. I know this place like I know my own eggs. And the name's Hoop. Oop-oop!"

— 3 Hoop &

"Well, I hope you'll help us out, Hoop-oop-oop," I said.

His head feathers rose in annoyance. "No, it's *Hoop.* Oop-oop!"

"That's what I said," I told him, a little annoyed myself. "Hoop-oop-oop."

"Ra, I think he's saying his name is Hoop," Miu murmured. "With no *oop-oop*."

"Then why didn't he say so?" I wanted to know.

"Ra, can we please get going?" Khepri mumbled from under my belly.

Hoop overheard him. "Sure thing, beetle-o!" Bobbing his long beak in my direction, he added, "So where do you want to go?"

The tantalizing smell of spiced beef reached my nose. "How about the banqueting hall?" I suggested.

"We were following Lady Satiah," Miu reminded me.

"And that's where she was headed," I reminded her. "Besides, I'm hungry. I haven't had a thing since that oxtail."

Hoop shot up, spreading his black-and-white wings wide. "Oop-oop! Follow me."

It turned out I was right, of course. Lady Satiah was already in the banqueting hall, along with her brother and the children. Scenting that fabulous spiced beef again, I scampered out to join them, only to stop in my tracks.

The floor was covered in crocodiles.

Painted crocodiles, I mean—but they startled me. More scaly portraits shimmered on the walls and curled around the doorways. It was almost enough to put me off my appetite . . . though not quite. The place smelled too good for that.

Ignoring the dubious décor, I surveyed the table. Where was my plate? I couldn't spot it anywhere, even when I jumped onto a high ledge for a better view.

Miu came with me. "What a feast!" she said, judging the table with her kitchen cat's eye. "The cooks must have been busy since dawn. It's a meal fit for a pharaoh."

"Probably because that's who Lady Satiah was planning it for." Khepri peered out from my belly fur. "No wonder she looks so annoyed. Half the food will go uneaten."

"Not if I have anything to do with it," I muttered.

I arranged myself in my finest Bastet pose, ready for a servant to bring me my share. I waited, and I waited. But to my horror, no one came.

"Royal or not, it looks like you're going to go hungry, oop-oop!" Hoop chuckled from an alcove above. "Better take another look at that beetle you're carrying. He could be just the nibble you need."

"Knock it off," I said. "I told you. He's my friend."

"Right," Hoop said. "I forgot. Oop-oop!"

Khepri ducked down into my fur again. As he did, my stomach growled. I needed food *now*. It was undignified for Pharaoh's Cat to have to beg for his supper, but I was desperate. I nuzzled up to Kiya and meowed.

"Oh, poor Ra-baby! Didn't they bring you any food?" Kiya picked up a cube of spiced beef from her plate. "Here, you can have this."

Before I could take it, Lady Satiah shooed

me away. "There are fish scraps at the zoo for your cats," she said coldly to Kiya.

Fish scraps! For Pharaoh's Cat! I almost retched.

Kiya looked sick, too. "Ra can't eat fish, Lady Satiah. They're unclean. Everyone in Pharaoh's court knows that."

"He's not a member of the royal family. He's a cat." Lady Satiah said *cat* as if it were *dung*. "If he's hungry enough, he'll eat anything."

What an insult! I retreated to the ledge where Miu sat.

"Outrageous!" I whispered. "I'm a royal, born and bred. And we don't eat fish."

"Well, kitchen cats aren't fussy," Miu said. "And I'm getting hungry. I wouldn't mind eating some fish at the zoo."

"I need a snack, too," Khepri put in. "And the zoo works for me."

"We should wait a bit," Miu said to Khepri. "I don't want to leave the children alone with Ra."

"What are you talking about?" I said. "I'm their guardian. It's Lady Satiah you should be worrying about. And maybe that brother of hers."

"I'm just saying that you aren't as vigilant as you could be," Miu said to me. "Like today on the boat."

"One tiny nap," I said indignantly, "and you—"

"Tiny!" Miu repeated. "Ra, it was hours."

"And even a tiny nap could be a problem," Khepri told me. "Miu's right. You never know when something is going to happen, so you need to—"

"A lion!" Hoop screamed, feathers aflutter. "Oop-oop! Prepare to be eaten alive!"

CHAPTER 6

Lion on the Loose!

I thought Hoop was kidding, but there really was a lion on the loose. He was only a cub, but he was fast. He sped through the banqueting hall, skidding on the tiles.

"Grab him!" Lady Satiah shouted at her servants.

The servants didn't exactly leap to the task.

"Whee!" The cub dashed past them, then glanced up at Miu and me. Under a mischievous tuft of hair, his eyes were bright. "Hey, cats! You want to play, too?"

Play with a lion cub? "Thanks, but we'll pass," I called out.

Luckily, the Keeper of the Zoo was on the cub's trail. Behind him were two men, armed with giant nets. One was tall, long-faced, and sniffly. The other was stocky and red-nosed.

"Sorry, my lady!" the Keeper puffed. "We'll have him out of here in a jiffy." He called out to the sniffly man. "Hormin, you approach from the left." Nodding at the red-nosed man, he added, "And Qen, you approach from the right."

Sniffly Hormin moved the fastest, but it was red-nosed Qen who netted the cub just before he reached the table. As the men carried their prize off, Lady Satiah snarled at them, "Don't let it happen again."

"Of course not, my lady." The Keeper bowed, then scooted after the cub.

Lady Satiah didn't cheer up after the cub was gone. She stared at her plate as her brother told long-winded tales about his military exploits.

"What a bore!" Hoop whistled. "That's General Wegaf. Made so many blunders in Nubia that he was dismissed. No surprises there. He can barely lead the way to dinner."

A servant came up to Lady Satiah and whispered in her ear.

"Oop-oop!" Hoop was still jeering at General Wegaf.

"What's that servant saying?" Khepri asked me.

"I can't hear." I glared at Hoop.

"Shhh!" Miu sat up on her haunches. "Pay attention, everyone. They're getting up. We'd better follow."

"Let's grab a snack first," I said, leaping for the table. But I'd hardly sampled Lady Satiah's leftovers when she said something that made me choke.

"The servants who came with you have fallen ill," she told Kiya and Dedi. "It must have been something they ate on the boat. They have been put in the sickroom. Never fear: my own servants will attend you."

"I don't like the sound of that," Khepri said.

I didn't, either. I leaped down from the table.

"You must give me your valuables," Lady Satiah ordered the children. She surveyed the considerable amount of gold, silver, and jewels that Kiya and Dedi were wearing. "You may keep your amulets, of course. I wouldn't want to deprive you of their protection. But your rings and cuffs and everything else must go into safekeeping for the night." She turned to an older man with a bald head and a pristine white tunic. "Steward, collect them in that basket over there. Then bring them to my bedroom for safekeeping."

"Safekeeping?" Hoop hooted. "Oop-oop! I bet those jewels will spend the night on Lady Satiah herself. That lady loves a bauble."

Kiya and Dedi couldn't understand a word of this, of course, and they were used to servants looking after their jewelry. Nevertheless, they were slow to hand their jewels over. But it was only when Lady Satiah sent them to their rooms that Kiya kicked up a fuss. "I want to stay with my brother."

"This is my palace, and you will sleep in the ladies' quarters," Lady Satiah said. "Now it's time for bed for you both, and for Ahmose, too. Come with me, Kiya. Dedi and Ahmose, you will go with Turo."

She directed Dedi toward a young man with tousled hair, who smiled and bowed to Dedi. "Most gracious son of the Ruler of

Rulers, I am Ahmose's tutor. Please follow me to your room."

"That Turo's a charmer, eh? Oop-oop!" Hoop chortled. "Shame he's got no gold. He'll spend his life serving Lady Satiah." He wheeled up to the ceiling. "Oh, well, time for me to catch some z's, too. See you later! Or not. Oop-oop!"

As the children headed off in different directions, Miu said, "We need to split forces. You two go with Kiya, and I'll go with Dedi."

"Oh, no," I said. I wasn't going to play dress-up all night. "You go with Kiya, and we'll go with Dedi." With Khepri clinging to my fur, I darted after Dedi.

"Stay alert!" Miu called after us. "He's the crown prince, remember. Don't let anyone pull any tricks on you."

"As if someone could!" I grumbled to Khepri as we followed Dedi to a bedroom near the great hall. "Miu seems to forget that I'm Pharaoh's Cat."

After Turo said good night, Dedi bedded down. Moonlight poured through a high window, revealing his worried face. I curled up next to his head.

"I hate it here," he told me. "I wish we were home. I'd go right now if I could . . ."

He yawned and turned over. I yawned, too.

"Don't get sleepy, Ra," Khepri warned from between my ears. "We've got a job to do."

"And I'm on it," I told him. "No matter how tired I am. Or how hungry."

"How can you be hungry?" Khepri asked. "You just ate."

"A mere smidgen, that's all I had," I told him. "I couldn't begin to do the meal justice. Really, it's agony thinking of it going to waste."

"Like that zoo," Khepri mused.

"What zoo?"

"The one here," Khepri said wistfully. "Think of the dung they must have, Ra. Crocodile. Lion. Antelope, maybe. Or gazelle. Could be ostrich, even. It's just lying there, with no one to eat it."

"Yuck!" I put my paws over my ears. "It's bad enough being hungry, Khepri. Don't make me sick, too."

The trouble with putting your paws over

your ears is that they muffle everything. And when it's dark and things are muffled, you can easily fall asleep. Which is what I did.

I guess Khepri did, too. Because the next thing we knew, it was morning, and Kiya was in the doorway, wailing, "Dedi's gone. He's disappeared!"

CHAPTER 7

Nightmare

Khepri and I stared at each other in dismay.

Miu bounded into the room behind Kiya. "Where is Dedi? Kiya dreamed that somebody kidnapped him, and she was so worried that it worried *me*. Please tell me nothing happened."

"Er . . . not as far as we know," I said.

Miu took a step back. "Oh, no. Don't tell me you both fell asleep!"

"Okay." I looked down at my paws. "We won't tell you."

"But that's what happened," Khepri said softly.

Miu closed her eyes.

"Let's not overreact," I said. "Maybe Dedi just got up early."

"He didn't," Miu said tightly. "Kiya asked the Steward. No one's seen him. They thought he was sleeping."

I felt a prickle of panic. Had something actually happened to Dedi—on my watch? The thought was so awful that I pushed it away. "Look, I'm sure he's around somewhere."

Kiya's wails grew louder.

"What is all this racket?" Lady Satiah appeared in the doorway, her wig askew and one lip redder than the other.

A tiny woman scampered after her, a paintbrush in her hand. "My lady, if I could finish your mouth . . ."

"Who's that?" Khepri asked me.

"Must be a Painter of Her Mouth." I

watched as the tiny woman darted toward Lady Satiah's lips with the brush. She squeaked in alarm as Lady Satiah swatted the brush away. "They do makeup for rich ladies."

Lady Satiah strode over to Kiya. "Your brother isn't here, you say? Well, stop belly-aching and go find him."

"I've looked." Kiya's tears welled up again. "He's gone. I had a dream that some-one kidnapped him, and it came true."

"Nonsense," Lady Satiah said. "No one

gets kidnapped in my palace. I would never permit it."

"Then where is he?" Kiya asked.

"We'll find out." Lady Satiah whirled around so fast that her wig slid over her eyebrows. With another squeak, the Painter jumped to straighten it.

"Steward!" Lady Satiah shouted.

The Steward appeared, rubbing at his just-shaved chin. His tunic was as perfectly white as Lady Satiah's own. "You called, my lady?"

"When did you last see the crown prince?" Lady Satiah demanded.

"I haven't seen him since last night, my lady."

"That's what everyone says." Kiya sounded desperate. "I asked people to help me find Dedi when I got up, because I didn't know where his room was. Everyone said he must be here. But he's not."

Frowning, Lady Satiah sat down on Dedi's rumpled bed. The Painter dashed over and painted her lower lip. When the brushwork was finished, Lady Satiah said, "It's probably some schoolboy joke."

"No, it's *not*," insisted Kiya. "He's in trouble. Somebody's captured him. That's what my dream told me. "When Lady Satiah didn't respond, Kiya's voice went up a notch. "You have to do something, Lady Satiah. You have to help me find him."

Lady Satiah gave her a cool look—like the look cats give to humans when they try to boss us around. But Kiya stood her ground. She was Pharaoh's daughter, after all.

After a long moment, Lady Satiah turned to the Steward and said, "Get to the bottom of this. Report to me in the great hall when you find the boy."

As she swept out, the Painter and the Steward bustling behind her, I stared at Dedi's bed.

"I have a bad feeling about this," I said.

"Me too." Khepri sounded very subdued.

"Well, don't let your feelings get in the way of your detective instincts," Miu warned. "We're on a case now."

"That's true." Khepri clicked hard, as if he were pulling himself together.

I tried to pull myself together, too. "Where do we start?"

"I'll stay with Kiya and make sure she's safe," Miu said. "You two search the palace. There are lots of places the humans won't think to look. Check them all."

Together, Khepri and I explored every inch of the main living quarters in the palace. Unfortunately, the palace cleaners had already washed the floors that morning.

Agitated, I stalked around a fancy suite of rooms near Dedi's bedchamber. "They swept away clues, and they destroyed the scent trails. It's a deliberate cover-up."

"I don't know, Ra." Seated by my ears, Khepri sounded doubtful. "More likely, they were just doing their jobs."

"It's a conspiracy," I insisted. "The whole palace is in on it."

"Let's not get ahead of ourselves," Khepri said. "We don't know for sure if Dedi is missing. And even if he is, the servants here are trying hard to find him. Look at those two guys over there."

I glanced at the men, who were opening the many decorated chests in the room to make sure Dedi wasn't inside. One man was tall, long-faced, and sniffly. The other was stocky, with a red nose. They looked familiar.

"They're the guys who caught the lion cub last night," Khepri whispered in my ear. "Remember? Hormin and Qen."

Qen yawned and rubbed his red nose. "Up all night guarding the palace, and now this," he said to Hormin. "We get the worst jobs around here."

"There are worse jobs than this," Hormin said with a sniff. "I should know. I've done some of them."

"Like what?" Qen wanted to know.

Hormin's long face drooped. "Like dung duty at the zoo."

"Dung duty sounds pretty bad," Qen agreed.

"Actually, it's my dream job," Khepri murmured.

"Next to that, night watchman is a piece of honey cake," Hormin went on. He levered the lid back onto a huge chest.

Qen leaned up against the wall and watched Hormin work. "It's not being night watchman that gets to me. It's being at her beck and call the rest of the day, too. And she's not the only one—"

"Stop the whining." Hormin banged the lid down. "We've got it pretty good here, if you ask me. So how about you quit complaining and help me? If the Steward catches you standing around when he's told us to look for that kid, there's going to be trouble."

"Okay, okay," Qen grumbled. "But I don't see why everybody in this palace thinks they can order us around. *Hormin and Qen, catch that lion cub. Hormin and Qen, go find the prince. Hormin and Qen—*"

"Hormin and Qen!" the Steward barked.

The two watchmen jumped to attention.

Frowning, the Steward hurried over to them. "Have you searched General Wegaf's rooms?"

"Not yet, my lord," Hormin said. "But we'll do that right away—"

"No, no!" the Steward cut in. "Lady Satiah says you're to leave him undisturbed. Now, if you've finished here—"

"We haven't," Qen told him.

"Well, I need to talk with you anyway," the Steward said. "I have some questions about last night."

Before I could hear the questions, Khepri's legs beat a sudden rhythm on my head. "Hey, Ra! There's Lady Satiah, and she's in a hurry."

I looked up in time to see Lady Satiah's beaded gown flashing past an archway.

"I bet she's up to something," I said. "Let's follow her!"

As everyone knows, Pharaoh's Cat has an unerring sense of direction. But some palaces are badly laid out, and that isn't my fault. Before I knew what was happening, I found myself trotting down a dingy passageway.

"Are we lost?" Khepri said as I slowed down.

"Pharaoh's Cat doesn't get lost," I told him. "I'm . . . er . . . getting my bearings."

"Better get them fast," Khepri warned me. "Here comes trouble!"

I turned and saw a lion cub galloping toward us.

CHAPTER 8

Kittycat

Lion cubs look awfully cute from a distance. Up close? That's a different story.

I ran around the corner, but the passage dead-ended at two shut doors.

"Hey, kittycat!" The cub careened toward me, his mischievous tuft of fur bobbing. "I sneaked out again when the Keeper of the Zoo was cleaning my cage. Let's play!"

"Er . . . let's not." Whatever the cub had in mind was going to be worse than dress-up. I sidestepped him—or tried to. But he thought that was part of the game.

"Tag!" he screeched. He head-butted me in the side, knocking me flat. That's the problem with cubs. They don't know their own strength.

Once I got my breath back, I let out a low warning cry, one step short of a snarl. Among us cats, big and small, that means "Don't touch me."

I guess the cub didn't know the code.

"You're funny, kittycat. Let's play family. You be the naughty cub, and I'll be the daddy lion." With a giggle, he grabbed me by the scruff of my neck.

Oh, the indignity! Pharaoh's Cat, being carted around like a kitten!

"Put . . . me . . . DOWN!" I gasped.

Instead, he shook me hard.

"Stop that!" I wailed. Forget my pride— now I was worried about my survival.

Just as I thought my teeth were going to be jangled out of my head, a door at the end of the passage opened. A young woman with a sweet face and drab clothes stared down at us.

"What—oh!" She knelt by the lion cub. "You silly baby. That's not a toy. That's a cat. And a very fine cat, too. Let him go."

She pulled the cub close. I guess that surprised him, because he dropped me right away.

"Poor cat." The young woman checked my neck with her free hand and said to the cub, "Well, at least you didn't leave a mark. Now let's get you back to the zoo."

I didn't wait to see them go. As soon as Khepri jumped back on, I scooted down the passageway.

Eventually, I found my bearings. When I reached the great hall, the Steward was bowing low to Lady Satiah. She was seated on her gilded chair, and her brother, General Wegaf, was standing alongside her.

With a nervous look at them both, the Steward bobbed up. "There's no sign of the boy anywhere, my lady. But the night watchmen have something to tell you."

Stepping forward in their workaday tunics, Hormin and Qen bent low. Hormin's sniffling echoed loudly in the tiled hall, while Qen's nose was redder than ever.

"Yes?" Lady Satiah prompted them. "Did you see the boy sneaking out last night?"

"My lady, we saw no one." Hormin tried

to stifle his sniffles. "Er . . . no one, that is, except for Yaba. She was sleepwalking near the gates just before dawn . . ."

"Yaba?" I whispered to Khepri. "Who's that?"

"I don't know," Khepri said in my ear.

General Wegaf frowned. "Yaba—is that the Pharaoh's newest wife?"

"The minor princess from that dinky province in Assyria, yes," Lady Satiah confirmed. "Her father married her to Pharaoh to seal a trade deal."

Oh, right. I'd heard about that. Pharaoh hadn't been happy when his ambassadors had told him the terms of the deal, and the Great Wife had hit the roof. But a deal was a deal, and it would have caused a lot of political tension to undo it. So Pharaoh had gone through with the wedding ceremony and then sent his new wife to live a long distance away.

"She's been trying to escape at least once a week since she got here," Lady Satiah went on. "It's so annoying. Not that she gets very far. The watchmen see to that." She turned to them again. "And you were on duty all night? You didn't doze off or stop for a snack, the way you did last week?"

"Of course not, my lady," Hormin said, sniffling again. "And we didn't stop for a snack last week. We heard a rustling in the kitchen, remember?"

"That's right," Qen put in, sounding a trifle offended. "We know our job."

Lady Satiah frowned. "Then why did you not see the boy?"

"We have our rounds," Qen reminded her. "We do a circuit of the whole palace."

"But then who guards the gates?" Lady Satiah wanted to know.

The Steward coughed. "Er . . . the crocodiles do. At least, that's what you said when I asked for more money to replace the guards we lost last year."

"Oh, yes." Lady Satiah touched her hand to the thick braids of her wig. "I'd forgotten. Well, it's true. Who's going to rob us with the crocodiles around?"

"You may be right, my lady," the Steward said. "But all the same, we need more watchmen. Last night is proof."

Pursing her lips, Lady Satiah waved a hand at the watchmen still bowed low before her. "So you saw Yaba. Anyone else?"

"No, my lady," Hormin said.

"But it looks like someone got past us," Qen added. "Maybe while we were escorting Yaba back to her room. Or maybe a little before that, when we had to check on General Wegaf."

Disconcerted, Lady Satiah turned to her brother. "On you, brother? Why?"

The General turned red as a rooster's wattle. "Spot of bother. Not worth discussing."

Lady Satiah glared at him. "Out with it. Now."

CHAPTER 9

A Trick

"Well, if you must know, I dreamed we were under attack," General Wegaf said gruffly to Lady Satiah. "Warriors to the right of us! Warriors to the left! I grabbed my spear, of course. Started to lay into them. Made a bit of noise, I guess. Guards came running."

"We thought he was dying," Hormin explained with an annoyed snuffle. "And we couldn't get the door open because he'd barricaded it."

"Old soldier's trick," the General said, looking pleased with himself.

"It kept us busy for a while, my lady." Qen rubbed his red nose. "So maybe that was when he got past us."

"The crown prince, you mean?" Lady Satiah said.

"Yes," Qen told her. "At least, we think that's who left the footprints we saw out by the river, on the landing."

"They were sandal prints, actually," Hormin put in. "I saw them, too. About the size a twelve-year-old would make."

"We spotted them earlier, when we were looking for the boy," Qen told Lady Satiah. "The landing is swept clean every evening, so they must have been made overnight."

"Why didn't you report this before?" Lady Satiah demanded.

"We did, my lady," Hormin said. "The Steward told us he would look into it, and he ordered us to search the south wing for the boy in the meantime."

Seeing Lady Satiah's frown of displeasure, the Steward said quickly, "My lady, I examined the landing myself, with great care. There were no other sandal prints, except for the ones the watchmen have told you about."

"But how could the boy have gotten out to the landing?" Lady Satiah wanted to know.

"You lock the gates at night, don't you? And carry the keys with you?"

The Steward tugged at his white tunic. "You may remember, my lady, that I mentioned several months ago that one of the locks was not catching properly? I suggested it should be replaced."

"And was it?" Lady Satiah said.

"You told me that it could wait, my lady," the Steward said, "since we are rather short of funds right now, owing to the zoo."

Lady Satiah pinched her lips even more tightly together. "And how many footprints were there?"

"Only two," the Steward said. "But I also discovered that one of the boats is missing. A small skiff."

"So the boy took it." Lady Satiah looked peeved. "I suppose it's some sort of prank."

"I'm afraid you may be right, my lady," the Steward said. "I spoke with Ahmose. He says he told the prince about the boats at dinner last night, and the prince boasted about his navigating skills."

"That sounds fishy to me," I whispered

to Khepri. "Dedi's got his faults, but he's not a boaster."

"He's proud of how he can handle a boat, though," Khepri pointed out. "Maybe that sounded like bragging to Ahmose."

"Perhaps he decided to find his own way home," General Wegaf said. "Not a wise move, with so many crocodiles hanging around, but boys will be boys."

"Dedi wouldn't do something that foolish," I told Khepri.

"I hope not." Khepri sounded worried. "But you remember what he said last night, don't you? How he'd go home right now if he could? What if . . . ?"

He trailed off, but I knew what he was thinking, because I was thinking it, too. My spirits plummeted.

Behind us, Kiya entered the great hall, Miu at her heels, both of them as quiet as shadows. They were just in time to hear Lady Satiah snap out new orders. "Steward, tell my oarsmen they are to find Ramses Dedumose and his boat. No doubt he is headed home, but they have more skill than he does. If they start immediately, they should catch up with him before he gets far. They are to escort him to his mother, with my compliments."

As the Steward strode away, Lady Satiah turned to General Wegaf with a scowl. "How dare that boy play such a trick on me? Making his own way home, indeed—"

"No!" Like a little bull, Kiya charged at the General and Lady Satiah. "That's impossible. My brother would never leave me. Not in this place. Never, never, never."

"She's right," I whispered to Khepri. "Dedi wouldn't leave her behind." I relaxed my tail in relief. It had been awful thinking about Dedi meeting up with crocodiles.

But if he hadn't left the palace, *where was he?*

Lady Satiah's bracelets jangled as she stared at Kiya's defiant face. "He would never leave you, you say? And yet he is gone. And the boat, too."

The Painter rushed into the room, her tiny features stamped with panic. "My lady!" she squeaked. "The jewelry. It's gone!"

"What jewelry?" Lady Satiah sat bolt upright. "What are you talking about?"

"The boy's jewelry." In tears, the Painter prostrated herself at Lady Satiah's feet. "It wasn't my fault, my lady. When the Steward brought the jewelry to your bedroom, I put it into two linen pouches, and I stowed them away for safekeeping. But now the pouch with the boy's jewelry is gone."

Spots of angry red appeared on Lady Satiah's cheeks. "You mean the boy sneaked in while I was sleeping and took it? He *robbed* me?"

"My brother is not a thief." Kiya's cheeks went as red as Lady Satiah's. "Even if he did take them, they're his, not yours."

"Oh, he took them, all right," Lady Satiah said grimly. "It's exactly the sort of trick he would play. On the last visit, he crept into my room and put a lizard in my bed."

"But that was my idea," Kiya said.

Lady Satiah glared at her. "Was it, indeed?"

"Dedi helped, though," Kiya added with a sob. "He always helps with things like that. And now he's gone. I just know he's been kidnapped, and you won't even send a message to Daddy—"

"Of course I will be sending a message to Pharaoh," Lady Satiah snapped. "What do you take me for?"

"A kidnapper!" Kiya wailed.

Lady Satiah paled. "How dare you speak to me like that!"

Kiya didn't stop. "You've done something

to Dedi, I know you have. You don't want him to be Pharaoh. You want Ahmose to take his place—"

"That's enough!" Lady Satiah flew up from her chair in a fury. "Pharaoh's Daughter, you cannot speak like that without consequences. I am sending you home."

CHAPTER 10

Homeward Bound

Kiya kicked and screamed, but Lady Satiah refused to change her mind. Everything was soon arranged. The nursemaid and guards, looking sick and wobbly, were ushered onto the barge. The Steward himself carried Kiya on board.

"Dedi!" she shouted from the railing. "Dedi, where are you?"

"We'll find him," I meowed to her from the landing, but seeing me only made her wail. I winced. Despite the dress-up nonsense, she was a good kid at heart, and I hated to see her so upset. I knew Pharaoh would be, too.

But then, Pharaoh would be even more upset about Dedi.

78

"Where is Miu?" I asked Khepri. Perched on my head, he had a better view of the scene.

"Here I am!" Miu bounded over to us, panting. "I found those sandal prints. They're the right size, but there's not much scent. And the prints are smudged, so it's hard to tell if they're from Dedi's sandals or some other pair."

"So we can't say for sure if he left or not?" Khepri said uneasily.

"No, we can't," Miu said. "So who is going with Kiya, and who is staying here? We need to decide—and fast."

"I'm staying here," I said. "I'll get a ride home with Pharaoh later."

Miu gave me a stern look. "You aren't just trying to avoid dress-up time with Kiya, are you?"

"Of course not," I said indignantly. "Dedi could be here, and it's my duty to find him. After all, he disappeared on my watch."

"It's my fault, too," Khepri piped up between my ears. "I'll help you search, Ra."

"Well, we can't let Kiya sail by herself," Miu said. "So if you're staying here, I'll go with her. With luck, I'll find Dedi safe at the other end."

As she headed for the gangplank, Khepri jumped down and settled himself between my paws. "So where do we start, Ra?"

Wasn't it obvious? "With breakfast, of course."

Khepri clicked at me in reproof. "You're supposed to be thinking about Dedi, not your appetite, Ra."

"I am thinking about him," I said. "But I think better on a full stomach. I bet they have leftovers from last night's feast in the kitchen. I'll get myself a quick snack and we'll be on our way."

With a sigh, Khepri hopped onto my head. "Well, if you're going to have breakfast, I guess I will, too. Stop by the zoo, and I'll get something to go."

"Not if you're getting a ride from me," I said. "You can eat it right there. And wipe your feet afterward."

"Okay, but we need to move fast," Khepri said. "It sounds like Dedi probably disappeared just before dawn. And that was only two hours ago. The trail is still hot."

"True," I agreed. "Luckily, we already know where the trail leads."

"We do?"

Khepri's a bright beetle, but sometimes he misses what's right under his antennae. "Sure we do," I said. "It leads straight to Lady Satiah. Didn't you hear what Kiya said? Lady Satiah kidnapped Dedi because she wants Ahmose to take his place."

"But it wouldn't work like that," Khepri said. "It's Pharaoh who decides who the crown prince will be. And if Lady Satiah kidnapped Dedi, Pharaoh would never choose Ahmose as his new heir. He probably wouldn't anyway, because it would make the Great Wife angry. She'd want one of her younger sons to inherit the throne."

Hmmmmm . . . I hadn't thought about that.

"And what about that missing boat?" Khepri added. "I know Kiya says Dedi would never leave this place without her. And she's probably right. But you remember what Dedi said when he was falling asleep, don't you? How the only good thing about being here was that they had so many boats?"

Uh-oh. I didn't remember Dedi saying that, but then, I'd had my paws over my ears. Not that I wanted to admit that to Khepri.

"So I worry that Dedi might have set out on a trip down the river, just for fun," Khepri went on. "I know he's good with boats, but these are the worst floods we've ever had. He could easily get washed up somewhere." He gulped. "Or even washed overboard."

Overboard was not a word I wanted to think about, so I was glad when Miu interrupted us. "Ra! Khepri!" She raced down the gangplank to the landing. "I have to talk to you."

"Don't miss your boat!" Khepri warned. "The sailors look like they're ready to go."

"Don't worry," Miu reassured him. "I've got a few minutes. They're still bringing food on board. The cook says a crate of meat on board has spoiled and needs to be taken away."

How spoiled? I wondered. If it was merely a touch, I wouldn't mind nosing around. "Thanks for the tip," I told Miu.

"That's not the tip," Miu said. "It's the crocodiles. I heard them splashing around as Kiya looked over the railing. *'Now there's a delicious morsel,'* one of them said. *'Just like the one who came out at dawn.'"*

I looked at her in horror. "They saw Dedi?"

"What if they *ate* him?" Khepri clacked in dismay.

It was starting to look like a possibility, and the thought was so terrible that I stopped feeling hungry. In fact, I stopped feeling pretty much anything.

"I hope I'm wrong." Miu's whiskers twitched anxiously. "But it didn't sound good. I yelled down to the crocodiles to get their attention, but they only laughed and swam away. They're still around, though. Well, one of them is, anyway. You can see him lying in the mud near the landing. He's the one with the huge ridges on his tail and the snout that's bigger than anyone else's."

I was starting to feel something now: *anger.* I gazed past the busy landing, where men were carrying crates on and off the royal barge, and scanned the riverbank. It took me a while, but I finally spotted Miu's crocodile.

He was the biggest, meanest crocodile I'd ever seen. Even bigger and meaner than the one that had lunged at Khepri and me the night before.

"I have to get back to Kiya," Miu said. "I led her to her cabin, but I don't know how long she'll stay there. It's up to you two to get that crocodile to talk."

"We'll make him talk." My fur bristled. "We'll go on the attack." I was so angry, I almost charged down to the riverbank then and there.

But then the crocodile opened his mouth wide. Even from this distance, I could see

his many, many teeth—and I felt something else: a cold trickle of *fear*.

I sat down hard. "Er . . . maybe I'll have breakfast first."

"Oh, Ra." Miu turned a disappointed gaze on me. "Does food always have to come first? I thought you were a Great Detective."

"Great Detectives need Great Snacks," I told her.

"Maybe you should be the one to go with Kiya," she said.

"No, you should," I said.

"No, you."

"But—"

"Hey, the barge is leaving!" Khepri broke in.

Miu careened down to the edge of the landing. I raced down with her, but it was too late. The barge was headed down the Nile, with Kiya on board—and without a single Great Detective to guard her.

CHAPTER 11

Great Detectives?

"Oh, no!" Her torn ear drooping forlornly, Miu stared at the widening gap between us and the barge. Ten cubits. Fifteen cubits. Twenty cubits.

I brushed up alongside her. There was something about the way she was standing that made me worry. "You can't jump that far, Miu. No cat can."

"Don't do it, Miu," Khepri put in.

Miu stayed put, but she didn't stop watching the barge, and now her whole head was drooping. "She's so small. Practically a kitten. And now she's on her own. We really messed up, getting distracted like that." As the barge glided away, she stared down at her paws. "*I* really messed up."

"You're not alone," Khepri said. "Ra and I didn't do a very good job of guarding Dedi, either."

"I guess we shouldn't call ourselves Great Detectives anymore," Miu said sadly.

I sat up straight. "Now, wait a minute. That kind of talk isn't going to get us anywhere."

"But it's true, Ra," Khepri said with a sigh. "Great Detectives don't let two children vanish."

"Kiya hasn't vanished," I pointed out. "We know exactly where she is. And she has guards and a nursemaid to protect her, even if they're under the weather."

"And Dedi?" Khepri buzzed.

"Well, that's more of a worry," I admitted. "But we've barely started detecting. And you can bet we have a better chance of finding him than anyone else does."

Miu perked up. "You're right, Ra. We need to focus on this case. And I know just where to begin." She started trotting down the landing.

"Where?" I called out.

She sped up. "That crocodile, of course!"

"No need to be so hasty!" I shouted after her. "Remember, we haven't even had breakfast yet. And maybe he hasn't, either!"

"She isn't listening, Ra." Khepri climbed onto my back. "We'd better go after her. You know how she can be with suspects."

I certainly did. Miu is a kindhearted cat, but put her in charge of an investigation and she acts like a lion. Still, even a lion isn't a match for a crocodile.

I caught up with her at the top of a landing wall covered with fishnets drying in the sun. Below us, the huge crocodile was clambering onto the muddy riverbank. I measured the distance down to the ground with my eyes. It was an easy jump for a cat—but not a wise one.

"Miu, you can't go down there!" Khepri warned. "He'll eat you."

The crocodile was already watching us, his golden-green eyes aware of our every move. He slithered closer to our spot on the wall.

"You better not have eaten Dedi, you big

bully!" Miu shouted down at him. "You'll be in trouble if you did. He's the crown prince of this whole kingdom, you know."

"Crown prince?" The crocodile's jaws snapped. "What do you know about that?"

It wasn't easy to understand him. Maybe it's all those teeth, but crocodiles have very poor enunciation, as you probably know if you've tried to talk to one yourself.

Not that I've ever complained to them about that. Nobody in their right mind complains to a crocodile about anything. Well, except Miu. But even she was looking daunted now that those snapping jaws were so close.

"Let me handle this," I said to her. "I've been trained for it."

It was true. I had been. Sort of. My father knew that when I succeeded him as Pharaoh's Cat, I would accompany Pharaoh on his Nile trips, so he'd warned me about crocodiles. *Always show respect,* he'd said. *After all, they've been in Egypt longer than the rest of us, except maybe the scarabs. They have their own rituals, and their own way of doing things. And they're very touchy.*

"O most noble and worthy crocodile," I began. "I am Ra the Mighty, Pharaoh's Cat, Lord of the Powerful Paw, and I greet you with—"

"Cut to the point," the crocodile growled. "What do you know about the crown prince?"

Hmmmmm . . . This encounter wasn't going the way I thought it would. But I decided to meet him on his level. (Not on the mudbank, of course. I mean his *conversational* level.) "No, you go first. What do *you* know?"

Miu scowled down at the crocodile. "Did you see the crown prince this morning? Did you eat him for breakfast?"

"What are you talking about, you stupid cat?" The crocodile thwacked his bumpy tail against the mud. "Why in Sobek's name would we eat one of our own?"

Miu and I sat back on our haunches, confused.

Up on my head, Khepri murmured, "Now that's interesting. You know, I—"

Without finishing his thought, he shrieked and slid down under my belly. I ducked my head down between my forelegs and peered at him. "Khepri? What is it?"

"Up there!" he croaked. "In the sky!"

Glancing up, I spotted the dirty feathers and bright-orange faces of vultures, soaring high above us.

"She's going to eat us," Khepri wailed.

"I thought vultures only ate carrion," Miu said. "You know, dead things?"

"Er . . . mostly," I said. "But they've been known to eat small animals."

"They eat insects, too," Khepri put in from under my belly. "And dung. Sometimes insects *and* dung. That's what happened to my cousin."

"Let's not get ahead of ourselves," I told him. "This one probably hasn't even noticed us. She might not even be hungry."

Letting out an excited hiss, one of the vultures dived for us.

"Sounds hungry to me!" Miu said.

"Run!" I shouted.

CHAPTER 12

A Deal's a Deal

Miu and I ran, all right—into each other. In our panic, we got caught in the fishing nets that were drying on the wall.

The vulture swooped down on us. Trapped on top of the wall, we were easy pickings. Kicking at the knotted strings only made the tangle worse. I ducked my head, waiting for the claws to sink in.

But instead of the rip and tear of talons, there was only a whistle of air. The vulture pulled up short, then touched down on the landing wall in front of me.

When I lifted my head up, the vulture was peering down at the crocodile.

"Hey there, Admiral," she croaked. "I

didn't see you at first. Are these friends of yours? I don't want to make a meal of your buddies."

"They're no friends of mine," the Admiral rumbled. "You can eat them if you want."

The vulture turned back toward me. Her eyes were bright and eager under her fringe of frilly head feathers. I struggled to free my paws from the net, but it was no use.

"I'm Ra the Mighty, Pharaoh's Cat," I babbled to the vulture. "Believe me, you really, really don't want to eat me. Or my friends."

"I'm Nekhbet," she said, drawing closer. "And believe me, I really, really do."

Kicking again at the nets, I got my forepaws free, but my hind legs were still trapped. "Sorry," I whispered to Khepri. "Run for it, if you can. I can't save us."

"But I can save *you!*" Khepri bounded out from my belly fur. Balancing on top of the nets, he shouted, "I know where the crown prince is!"

"What?" Miu said.

"Where?" I said.

"Who?" Nekhbet said. She waddled after Khepri.

"Khepri, watch out!" I clawed at the netting. My desperation to save him must have given me strength, because this time I managed to slice through the string and free myself. I bolted for Khepri, reaching him moments before Nekhbet did.

"Khepri, buddy, where's Dedi?" I panted.

"Not that prince," Khepri said. "The other one."

He'd lost me. "*What* other one?"

"You crocodiles have a crown prince, don't you?" Khepri called out to the Admiral. "That's the one I'm talking about."

"You've seen little Sobek Junior?" Nekhbet darted closer. "Why didn't you say so before? We've been looking everywhere for him. That cutie-pie likes to climb high on the riverbanks to sun himself, and that's not safe for a little crocodile. He's been gone for two days now."

Down on the mudbank, the Admiral had risen up on his stumpy front feet. "Where is our prince? What have you done with him?" His lizardy eye glared at us. "Did you eat him?"

"Of course we haven't eaten him!" Khepri hopped as he made his point. "But I think I know where he is."

I tried to look like I was in on the secret, but I was clueless. Crocodile prince? All I'd seen were these huge granddaddy-sized lizards out on the Nile. Well, except for that crocodile baby on Lady Satiah's—

Oh.

"I know where he is, too," I called down to the Admiral.

"And so do I," said Miu, who finally had freed herself from the netting. "And if you're nice to us, we might even help you get him back."

"Nice?" Nekhbet waddled toward us. "I'll give you nice. A nice peck on the patootie!"

The Admiral lashed his tail. "Knock it off, Nekhbet. If they know something, we'd better hear it. We need all the help we can get. King Sobek is going to chew my head off if I don't find Sobek Junior soon."

So there was an even bigger, scarier crocodile somewhere on this river? I gulped.

"We'd better tell them everything we know," I whispered to Khepri.

But Khepri had other ideas. "Sure, we'll help you," he called down to the Admiral. "But first you have to help us. We've got a missing prince of our own—a boy about twelve years old. He might have come down to the river right before dawn, and he maybe went out in a small boat. Did you see him?"

The Admiral shut his eyes and sank back down into the oozing mud.

"You ate him!" Miu cried. "I knew it!"

The golden-green eyes flashed open. "Hold your horses. I'm just thinking. Yes, there was a human out on the landing around first light. And he did mess around with the boats."

"How old was he?" I asked. "What did he look like?"

"Who knows? A human's a human." The Admiral grinned. "We don't keep track of their ages. We don't even look at their faces. We only care about how they taste."

"*A delicious morsel*," Miu said, looking sick. "That's what you called him."

"You heard that?" The Admiral's own earflaps went up—a sign of annoyance in a crocodile. "That was just one of my captains joking around. We saw a human come down to the dock, that's all. We might've eaten him if he'd fallen in, but he didn't."

"Did he go out in one of the boats?" Khepri asked.

"Who knows?" the Admiral said. "I'm not paid to keep tabs on humans. Anyway, we crocodiles were busy then. We always are, at dawn."

"Busy doing what?" Khepri wanted to know.

"Well, who do you think makes the sun come up?" the Admiral said. "The crocodiles, that's who."

Khepri wriggled his antennae. "But that's ridicu—"

"—really wonderful of you," I interrupted, nudging Khepri back. Never insult a crocodile.

"You bet it's wonderful," the Admiral snapped. "But don't think flattery is going to get you out of our deal. I helped you, and now you'd better help me. Tell me where Sobek Junior is."

Khepri tiptoed closer to the edge of the landing and peered down at the Admiral's scaly head. "We're pretty sure Lady Satiah has him."

"Lady Satiah!" the Admiral roared. "That vulture!"

"Ahem," said Nekhbet.

"You're right," the Admiral said. "Vulture's too good a word for that human. Is

 100

she planning to roast our crown prince in her kitchen?"

"Actually, I think he's part of her zoo," Khepri said.

"They've got a zoo at the palace?" The Admiral blinked, then glared up at the vulture. "Why didn't you tell me, Nekhbet? That should've been the first place we looked."

"I didn't know she had a zoo," Nekhbet said. "Maybe that's why she's put netting over the courtyards. You have to get real close to see through it, and I can't afford to do that, not when she's ordered her guards to shoot arrows at any vultures they see."

The giant crocodile paced along the mudbank, gnashing his teeth. "So close, and yet we can't get to him. Not unless the river floods the palace. Then we can break in. But it usually doesn't."

"Never mind, Admiral," Nekhbet comforted him. She swept her wings in our direction. "Remember, these animals promised to get him out for you."

"We did?" I said.

"No, we didn't," Khepri said.

"Well, I said we might *help*," Miu told the Admiral. "But I figured you'd be the one leading the expedition. I mean, we're strangers here. We can't—"

She stopped short as Nekhbet swung her sharp beak toward us. "A bargain is a bargain," she croaked. "Betray the crocodiles, and you'll regret it."

"You sure will," the Admiral snarled. "We'll lay the crocodile curse on you." He pointed his long snout at us and opened his toothy mouth wide.

I wasn't sure exactly what the crocodile curse was, but I had a bad feeling it involved teeth.

"No need for any curses," I said hastily. "Pharaoh's Cat is at your service. And so are his friends. We'll do everything we can to get your crown prince back to you."

"But we can't get anything done from here," Miu pointed out.

"And we could work faster if we weren't so worried about our own crown prince," Khepri added. "We've heard a boat went missing last night. If you could check downriver, and see if our prince is in it—"

"Sure," the Admiral agreed, with surprising enthusiasm. "We'll do that."

"And if you find him, don't eat him," Miu added fiercely.

The Admiral snorted. "I could say the same to you about our prince."

"No worries there," I said. "I don't even *like* crocodile."

The Admiral thwacked his tail against the mud. "Cut the wisecracks, cat. This is a serious situation. We've got a deal, and you'd better live up to it. "

"Don't worry. We're on it." Khepri jumped onto my back. "Come on, Ra. We've got a crocodile to rescue."

Even before he'd scrambled up to his perch between my ears, I was carefully picking my way around the nets. Miu was by my side, and within moments we were running over the bridge to the palace gates.

But it was the Admiral who had the last word.

"Remember, a deal's a deal," he snarled. "If I find your prince, and you don't bring back mine, then as far as I'm concerned, it's snack time."

CHAPTER 13

Don't Lose Your Nerve

Usually, I love to hear the phrase *snack time*. But it's not as appealing when a crocodile says it.

As we passed through the palace door, Miu sounded rattled, too. "Yikes! It's bad enough that we lost Dedi. Now we have to worry about that horrible crocodile making a meal of him. We'd better get to the zoo and figure out how to free Sobek Junior."

"I just hope Dedi hasn't been eaten by a crocodile already," Khepri fretted. "I don't think the Admiral was telling us the whole truth. He was awfully shifty. And that stuff about making the sun come up? Clearly nonsense. I mean, it's the scarab beetles who do that—"

"And Ra, the sun god, of course." I stopped in the great hall to get my bearings. "But crocodiles are odd creatures, Khepri. They have their own rites and rituals. And if they think they make the sun rise, it doesn't mean they're lying. Right, Miu?"

"I don't know." Miu flicked her ears uncertainly. "But I really hope no one's eaten Dedi."

I couldn't bear to think about that possibility. "Well, I think the Admiral was telling the truth. Anyway, it's not like we don't have an obvious suspect already."

Miu tilted her head. "Who?"

"Lady Satiah, of course. Remember what she was like when we arrived last night? How she glared at Kiya and Dedi? I thought she was going to unleash that baby crocodile on them."

Khepri clicked in my ear. "Speaking of baby crocodiles, we need to head for the zoo."

"I would, if I knew where the zoo was," I said.

Khepri swiveled around on the top of my head. "If I'm not mistaken, it's up on the right. There's a tasty scent of dung—"

"Enough said," I told him.

As Miu and I made tracks toward a passageway on our right, Khepri said, "I agree that Lady Satiah isn't a nice host, Ra. But we've had this discussion. If she kidnapped Dedi, Pharaoh wouldn't let her benefit. He'd send her and Ahmose into exile, and she's smart enough to know that."

"Only if he found out," I argued. "Maybe the missing boat is a decoy. Maybe Lady Satiah paid a servant to cut it loose, so that it would look like Dedi ran away. That way Pharaoh will end up blaming Dedi, not her."

"I don't know about that," Miu said. "I think there would be plenty of blame to go around. Anyway, I don't see how Lady Satiah could have made those footprints."

"Have you looked at her feet?" I said. "They're pretty small."

"It still sounds farfetched to me," Khepri said.

"Shhh!" I pulled into the shadows behind a painted pillar and flattened myself against the floor. "She's coming this way!"

Sure enough, Lady Satiah was headed toward us. Her bracelets and beaded collar chimed like delicate bells, but her gaze was flint-hard as she looked up at her companion.

"It's her brother," Khepri breathed into my ear. "General Wegaf."

It certainly was, but it took me a moment to recognize him. His military bearing had collapsed, and he seemed to have shrunk by several inches.

"I don't see how we can pull this off now," the General quavered. "Not when—"

"Don't lose your nerve," Lady Satiah whispered, her ruby lips mere inches from his ear. "Not when our plans are about to bear fruit."

"But Pharaoh—"

"I will deal with Pharaoh in my own way," Lady Satiah said.

"And the boy—"

"I will deal with that, too," Lady Satiah told him. "I have everything in hand. All I ask is that you support me. You want to stand at the head of an army again, don't you? Pull yourself together!"

She jabbed him in the back of the spine.

He shot up like a puppet, and she marched him off.

There was a long silence after they left.

"Okay," Khepri said in a small voice. "So maybe I was wrong about Lady Satiah."

"I told you she was guilty," I said.

"You didn't mention that she was working with her brother," Khepri said.

"That was sort of implied," I told him.

Miu shivered. "What do you think those plans of hers are?"

"I don't know," Khepri admitted. "But it could be pretty serious."

"Of course it's serious," I said. "It's a kidnapping."

"Oh, that's serious, all right," Khepri agreed. "Especially for Dedi. But that might not be the end of it." His voice grew quiet as a whisper. "What if Lady Satiah is planning to topple Pharaoh from his throne?"

"She wouldn't!" Shocked, I sank to the floor. "She couldn't!"

"Oh, I think she could," Khepri said. "Think about it. Remember, something kept Pharaoh in Thebes. Something important. What if he heard a rumor of a plot against him? Maybe that's why he wanted the children to be sent home. Only it turns out Lady Satiah is at the center of the plot, so he sent them to the worst possible place."

"But Lady Satiah is Pharaoh's wife," I protested. "She wouldn't go so far—"

"It's been done before," Khepri said grimly. "I heard about it from a horse in Pharaoh's stables. Once there was a pharaoh's wife—a lesser wife, just like Lady Satiah—who wanted her own son to sit on the throne. The pharaoh ended up dead."

"Well, that's not going to happen to my pharaoh," I said. "Or to Dedi. I won't allow it."

"I'm with you, Ra." Miu brushed her tail against mine. "And I think there's still time to stop her. Did you hear how she said she would 'deal with' Dedi? Sounds to me like Dedi is alive. Probably somewhere close, where she can get to him easily."

"Well, he's not in the main part of the palace," I said. "We checked everywhere."

"What about the zoo?" Miu suggested. "Judging from the smell, that's where Lady Satiah and the General were coming from."

I scrambled to my feet. "Let's go!"

As we raced down the gloomy passageway, the air got stinkier.

"Wow-ee!" Khepri bounced on my fur.
"It's like ten stables put together."

"Make that twenty," I panted. By now, the
air was so thick and musty I could barely
breathe. I started hearing strange noises,
too—squawks and growls and screeching.

Miu leaped forward. "We're getting close.
There's the entrance!"

I was so light-headed from the dung that
I missed the turn. Instead of swerving to
the left with Miu, I shot forward toward a
black hole in the floor.

When I caught a whiff of what was
ahead, I tried to claw to a stop, but I was
going too fast.

"Dung ho!" Khepri crowed.

"Noooooooooooooo!" I cried.

The world's biggest dung pit was straight
in front of me—and I was about to topple in.

CHAPTER 14

Royal Son of the Pharaoh

I scrabbled. I rolled. And I halted at the very edge of the dung pit.

"Hey, Ra!" Clinging to my ear, Khepri peered down into the pit. "Why did you stop? It's like a gold mine down there."

"A dung mine," I mumbled, my belly flat on the floor. "Lucky us."

"You said it," Khepri agreed with a happy sigh. "I've never seen anything like it. It's making me woozy."

I'd gone way past woozy—straight to sick.

Khepri peered over my brow. "Why, you haven't even opened your eyes, Ra. Come on. Take a look."

The stench was so bad I could barely

bring myself to glance down. When I did, the view was dizzying. The pit's brick walls, edged with dung, went down into darkness, like a tomb shaft. Squinting, I saw a dark mix of dung and water at the bottom.

"Makes you feel like going for a swim, doesn't it?" Khepri said.

"Khepri, have you lost your marbles? Even if I wanted to float in dung, which I don't, we'd never be able to get back up again."

"Why would you want to?" Khepri peered down the shaft again. "I've never seen such a great breakfast."

"You can dine elsewhere." I backed away from the pit edge.

"What are you doing over here?" Miu trotted up to us, whiskers twitching. "It stinks."

"We found a dung pit!" Khepri announced. "A huge one!"

"Um . . . great," Miu said. "I found the zoo. Come on."

She led us toward a gated archway. Through the bars, I glimpsed a large courtyard full of cages. But before I could see inside them, a door beside me opened and the Keeper came out.

His wrinkled face puckered at the sight of us. "Oh, dear. I can't have you terrorizing my birdies, cats. Shoo!"

Shoo? Didn't he know the rules? *If you wouldn't say it to Pharaoh, don't say it to Pharaoh's Cat.* I stood my ground . . .

. . . until the Keeper picked up a broom.

"Go on." His bushy white brows frowned anxiously as he swept the broom toward us. "Get out of here. Scat! Leave my birdies alone!"

I dashed toward the door he'd left open.

"No!" He swooped down with the broom again. "That's the storeroom. You don't belong there, either."

Pharaoh's Cat knows an invitation when he hears one. I ducked between the Keeper's legs and dashed into the storeroom, which ran between the dung pit and the zoo itself. It was packed as tight as the hold of a ship. Bowls and pails were stacked on shelves. A long wall was lined with huge bins. There was even a row of empty birdcages lined up above the door. It was all neat as could be.

Perfect.

"What are you doing?" Khepri shouted into my ear.

"I'm teaching that Keeper a lesson," I said. "Hold on!"

The Keeper chased me round and round the storeroom, but I've had lots of practice playing tag with Kiya, so I had the upper hand. All he did was make the place a mess.

THUMP went the broom.

WHOOSH-BAM went a basket, scattering birdseed everywhere.

CLATTER-SMASH went a pot, falling on a bin lid.

The whole room started to rattle. It was like being inside a drum.

Khepri's voice was so faint I could barely hear him. "How long is this lesson going to last, Ra? I'm getting seasick."

"No problem, buddy." I dashed back through the door to Miu, waiting behind a barrel.

"Having a good time?" she asked.

"The best," I told her.

The Keeper emerged from the storeroom, breathing heavily and brandishing his broom. He looked up and down the pas-sageway, but he didn't spot us.

"Darn cats," he muttered. As footsteps pattered closer and Ahmose came into sight, the Keeper straightened. Turo, the tutor, was right behind Ahmose, yawning.

"Hello there, young Ahmose!" The Keeper raised the broom handle in greeting. "You haven't seen any cats around here, have you?"

"I saw a couple last night at dinner," Ahmose said. "I think Dedi said they were Pharaoh's Cats."

Pharaoh's *Cats*? I glanced at Miu, who had a big cat grin on her face.

"You shouldn't call him Ahmose," the tutor corrected the Keeper. "His gracious mother commands us to refer to him as Royal Son of the Pharaoh."

"Does she now?" the Keeper said. "That's new."

The tutor shrugged. "It's what she wants."

"So what does that make you?" the Keeper asked him. "Royal Tutor to the Royal Son of the Pharaoh?"

The tutor laughed. "No. I'm just Turo."

"Well, you look tired, Turo," the Keeper said.

"I'm fine." Turo smothered another yawn. "But what is that awful smell?"

"That's the dung pit." The Keeper leaned his broom against the wall. "I was sure I closed it up after I pushed the last load in, but I guess I forgot. I'd better take care of that." He walked toward the pit. "Now, don't you two follow me. You don't want to fall in."

"I wouldn't mind," Khepri said softly.

I heard a scrape and a bang. "There, that's better," the Keeper said, coming back. "So what brings you here, Ahmose? Er . . . I mean, Royal Son of the Pharaoh."

"Ahmose is fine," the boy said. "Turo, you can call me Ahmose, too. After all, you're my cousin."

"Wait, they're cousins?" I whispered to Miu and Khepri.

"You can sort of see a resemblance," Miu whispered back. "Around the nose."

I looked, and it was true. Turo and Ahmose had the same beaky nose, in different sizes.

"I want to see the baby crocodile again," Ahmose told the Keeper.

"Oh, dear." The Keeper's wrinkles deepened. "I'm sorry, Ahmose, but that's not possible."

Ahmose pouted. "But I'm the one who caught him. You said he was mine."

"I did, I did. But there's a problem." The Keeper looked around, then bent toward the boy and whispered, "The baby crocodile is missing."

CHAPTER 15

A Classy Café

"Uh-oh." Khepri clicked in alarm.

Hidden behind the barrel, Miu and I stared at each other.

"I don't believe it," I said. "Another crown prince just slipped out of our paws?"

Miu hung her head. "What are we going to tell the crocodiles?"

"Shhh!" Khepri said. "Listen to what the Keeper's saying."

The Keeper was talking to Ahmose. "I'm telling you, that little crocodile was here when I went to bed. This morning, his cage was still locked, but he was gone."

Ahmose's cheeks were pale. "Did he slip through the bars?"

"I thought he was too big for that," the Keeper said, "but I guess I was wrong. Crocodiles can be tricky that way."

"And other ways, too," I added under my breath.

"Shhh!" Khepri said again.

Ahmose looked up at the Keeper. "Did you tell my mother that the crocodile is missing?"

The Keeper gulped. "Er . . . no. I thought maybe we'd keep that news to ourselves for now. Your very gracious mother seems upset this morning, so I thought I would look around first before I bother her. Starting here in the zoo."

"A wise plan," Turo agreed. "Lady Satiah has enough to worry about right now."

Ahmose stepped up to the gate in the archway. "How about we help you search for him?" he said to the Keeper.

"Good idea," I murmured. It would save us a lot of trouble if Ahmose found him.

"Maybe he'll even find Dedi, while he's at it," Khepri agreed.

Actually, I wanted to be the one to find Dedi. But to do that, we had to get past the gate and into the zoo.

"Ahmose, he's a very sweet baby crocodile, but he does have teeth," the Keeper warned. "I'm not sure about having you search for him."

"He won't bite me." Ahmose lifted the latch. "He knows I'm his friend. It's kind of like you and elephants."

The Keeper got a dreamy look in his eyes. "Oh, elephants are wonderful creatures, Ahmose. Did I ever tell you that the first zoo I worked in had one?"

Ahmose swung the zoo gate open. "You mean the one who curled his trunk right around your hand?"

"That's the one," the Keeper said, walking into the zoo with Ahmose. "Sweetest baby elephant you ever did see."

"With thick black lashes, right?" Ahmose said.

"Thickest I ever saw," the Keeper said. "I decided, then and there, that I was going to have my own elephant one day."

"That's just like me and my crocodile," Ahmose said.

Yawning again, Turo followed them through the gate, letting it fall shut behind him. "Now, Ahmose, you need to be careful . . ."

"Quick!" Khepri tugged my ear. "Turo didn't latch the gate. We can get in!"

As Miu and I pawed the gate open, we heard Ahmose say to the Keeper, "You never got an elephant of your own, did you?"

"Not yet, Ahmose, but I haven't given up hoping . . ."

It only took us a moment to squeeze through the gate. Avoiding the humans, we dashed down the first row of cages, then came to a stop. The place was packed, and everyone seemed due for a cage cleaning.

"It's more crowded than I expected," Miu said.

"And smellier," I added.

The smell didn't bother Khepri, though. "Now let's see if we can find Sobek Junior," he said into my ear. "And Dedi, too."

"And maybe some breakfast," I said faintly. I knew finding Dedi was important—every hour he was gone, my spirits sank a little more—but that game of tag in the storeroom was catching up with me. "All this running around on an empty stomach isn't good for me."

"Well, we've come to the right place." Khepri sniffed the air, then crawled over to a scrap of dung on the stone floor. "Wow! Gazelle dung. This sure is a classy café."

"Only if you're a dung beetle," I said miserably. "If you're a cat, not so much."

"Speak for yourself," Miu said beside me. "I smell fish." Poking her head into some pots that were lined up for feeding time, she emerged with a silvery tail sticking out of her mouth. "Mmmmmmm!"

"Yuck." I turned away, disgusted. I was hungry, all right, but Pharaoh's Cat has standards. I'd never stoop to eating food that Pharaoh and his family considered unclean.

As Miu slurped her fish down, I stalked a little farther into the zoo. The farther I went, the worse it stank, and no wonder. There were at least twenty cages here, wedged into a courtyard that wasn't much bigger than Lady Satiah's great hall. The ceiling was a patchwork of nets, which let some of the stench rise but did nothing to block the glare of the sun.

Despite the heat and the smell, I was hungry. Ducking into a tiny patch of shade beside an ibis cage, I licked my lips and surveyed the zoo again. There had to be something here that I could eat.

"My babies!" the white-feathered ibis shrieked.

I took a close look at her three tiny hatchlings. Was she offering her young for my hour of need . . . ?

The ibis's curved black beak sliced through the gap between the bars of the cage. "You've eaten my babies!" she screamed.

I drew myself up in my most dignified pose. "My dear lady, I didn't touch your babies." *Though I wouldn't mind a little roast ibis in pepper sauce . . .*

She turned a hysterical eye on me. "Not you. It's those greedy lion cubs. Though now that you mention it, I don't like the look of you, either." She spread her black-tipped wings over her hatchlings. "Stay away from my babies! Stay away!"

"Oh, give it a rest, why don't you?" the lioness growled from her cage across the way. "I'm tired of listening to your lies." She nuzzled her four cubs. "My darlings couldn't care less about your gawky little hatchlings. Who wants a mouthful of feathers and beak?"

"They ate my babies!" the ibis shrieked again. "I had five, and now I only have three."

"Maybe you miscounted," the lioness sniffed. "You silly thing."

"There were FIVE," the ibis insisted. "Five before we were captured, and five after. One, two, three, four, five. Until your nasty cubs slipped out of their cage and came looking for a meal—"

"Nasty?" the lioness growled. "You take that back, you flimsy bag of feathers! My sweet cubs never touched your wretched hatchlings. If you want to know who was to blame, it was probably that baby crocodile. He could gobble up your lot in one bite."

"The baby crocodile?" I darted over to the lioness's cage. "You saw him get out?"

Miu joined me, Khepri riding on her back. "Did he escape last night?" she asked the lioness.

"Did you see where he went?" Khepri wanted to know.

"We're looking for a boy, too," I added. "Not Ahmose. Another boy, even taller, with skinny legs."

The lioness ignored us. "I've had enough of these stupid accusations," she growled at the ibis. "Between you and that moaning gazelle over there, my darlings can hardly get a wink of sleep."

"My babies!" The ibis was screaming again. "You ate my babies!"

"If you could just answer our questions," I said to the lioness.

"Please," Miu told her. "It's terribly important—"

"Shut up, all of you!" the lioness roared.

The air shivered with the ferocious sound. We all took a big step back.

"Uh-oh." Khepri gave a nervous click from Miu's back. "I think the Keeper noticed that. He's coming over. We'd better move fast, or he'll throw us out!"

CHAPTER 16

Taweret

The Keeper wasn't too quick on his feet. By the time he reached the lioness, Miu and Khepri had found a hiding spot behind some buckets, and I was pressed close beside them.

"What is it, my lovely?" the Keeper crooned to the lioness. "What's upsetting you?"

"That loudmouthed ibis," she growled. "And there are a couple of cats and a beetle who should get lost, too."

Luckily, the Keeper didn't understand any of that. And neither did Ahmose or Turo.

"Maybe she's hungry?" Ahmose suggested.

"Could be," the Keeper said. "I've got some meat for her." A pail scraped. "Let's throw it in."

There had been meat right there, and I'd missed it? Antelope stew, maybe, or a scrap of glazed duck? I edged out from behind the buckets, just in time to see the food go flying into the lioness's cage.

"Uggh!" I pulled back fast. "That meat is raw."

Miu looked amused. "That's how lions like it, Ra."

"Well, they're welcome to it." I thought longingly of that glazed duck I'd imagined. Now that was a meal.

Yet even though I didn't think much of the lioness's palate, I had to admire her single-minded focus on her food. Peeking out again, I saw how quickly she tore into the meat. Her cubs were pouncing on it, too—all except one of them.

"Hey." Khepri jumped down from Miu's back. "Isn't that the cub who wanted to play with you, Ra?"

"You're right." I recognized the tuft of fur. The cub's mischievous glint was gone, though, and he was slumped on the cage floor. "Is he sick?"

"He sure looks like it," Khepri said. "I hope it's not because he ate Sobek Junior last night."

Yikes! I hoped not, too.

"What's the matter with that cub?" Ahmose asked the Keeper.

"The little fellow in the corner, you mean? Now that you mention it, he does look a bit down in the mouth." The Keeper stooped to have a closer look. "We'd better put him where we can keep a closer eye on him. Let me get a basket so we can carry him without getting clawed."

He went into the storeroom and came out with a large lidded basket in hand.

"We'll have to do the next bit fast." Opening the basket, the Keeper handed it to Turo. "Ahmose, stand back."

While the lioness was occupied with her meat, the Keeper cracked open the cage door, grabbed the cub, and slammed the door shut. Plopping the cub into the basket, he shoved the lid down and took the basket back from Turo.

The lioness snarled. "My baby! Bring him back, you kidnappers!"

"Serves you right!" the ibis screamed. "Now you'll know how it feels!"

"My baby!" The lioness threw herself at the barred door. "My sweet baby!"

"We'll put him in a separate cage," the Keeper said to Ahmose. "Right next to the one where your crocodile was. Come and see."

"He's headed to the scene of the crime!" Excited, Khepri scrambled up my back and bounced to the top of my head. "If we follow him, maybe we'll see some clues that everyone's overlooked. And then maybe we can find Sobek Junior."

"Maybe," I agreed. "Anyway, it beats trying to talk to a screaming ibis."

We crept after the Keeper, staying close to the ground so no one would notice us. No human, that is. There wasn't much we could do about the animals.

"Cats?" said a tired gazelle as we passed.

"Cats!" squawked the ibis.

"Two cats and a beetle!" shouted the monkeys.

Ignoring them, the Keeper stopped by a small pool with high walls. Next to it was a cluster of empty cages. "Here we are. In you go, little one." He tipped the cub into one of the cages and locked him inside.

"Mama," the cub whined. "I want my mama."

"We'll look after you, don't you worry." The Keeper soothed him. "And we'll get you something to eat and drink."

"I can get the water," Ahmose offered enthusiastically.

"And then we have to go," Turo told him.

"We need to get some lessons done."

Ahmose groaned, but Turo refused to back down. After the cub was fed and watered, they left. The Keeper stayed till the cub fell asleep, then wandered off as well, mumbling something about the dung pit.

Finally, the Great Detectives were in charge of the scene.

"So which one was Sobek Junior's cage?" Khepri asked.

I nosed around. There were three empty cages right near the one with the lion cub, but only one of them smelled even the faintest bit like crocodile. "I think this is it," I said, putting my head through the bars.

"I agree," said Miu. "But they must have washed it down since this morning. There's not much scent here. Nothing that gives us any clues, anyway."

I sniffed again. Miu was right.

Just as I was starting to feel discouraged, a deep voice vibrated like a gong at our backs. "Hey, you cool cats. What's going down?"

Turning, I saw an enormous creature rising from the muddy walled-in pool behind us. Water poured off her great gray back and down her vast snout, flowing like a waterfall over her giant flared nostrils.

"It's a hippo," Khepri whispered in awe.

I was pretty awed, too. I'd seen hippos now and then on the Nile, but I'd never come across one in a zoo before. And it's only when you see one out of the water that you realize how big they are.

I reminded myself that, in his own way, Pharaoh's Cat is awfully big, too—in presence, poise, and personality, if not in pounds.

"I'm Ra the Mighty, Pharaoh's Cat, Lord of the Powerful Paw," I said. "And these are my friends Khepri and Miu. We're Great Detectives."

The hippo plodded over to us, one wrinkled mountain of a foot at a time.

"I'm Taweret," she said pleasantly. "And I'm the only hippo in this zoo." Her eyes fluttered with pride. "Well, until my baby comes. Which won't be long now."

"You have our heartiest congratulations,"

TAWERET

Khepri assured her. "We're looking for a baby ourselves—a baby crocodile."

The hippo flapped a tiny ear. "You mean the one that was here? He's gone."

"So we've heard," Miu said. "We tried asking some of the other animals if they'd seen him, but they weren't much help. But maybe you—"

"My babies!" the ibis shrieked behind us. "They've been eaten!"

"My cub!" the lioness roared. "He's been stolen!"

"They go on like that all day long," Taweret told us. "What a drag, huh? Honestly, this is the noisiest place I've ever lived."

"It must be a big change from the Nile," Miu sympathized.

"I wouldn't know," Taweret said. "I've always lived in zoos—but they were *peaceful* zoos. Given how much they paid for me, I figured this zoo would be pretty mellow, too. Especially when it has such a nice Keeper. But the animals here are so uptight. Someone's always shouting that their babies are threatened. And then the whole place falls apart."

Sure enough, the cries were spreading from cage to cage.

"Calm down, everyone!" Taweret's bellow wasn't the equal of the lioness's roar, but it was impressive all the same. "Look, I get that it's a downer when bad stuff happens, but getting worked up about it doesn't help anyone. Tune in to the rhythm of life, and stop taking everything so personally, okay? Maybe your babies wandered off to get some peace and quiet. Think like an earth mother, and try a soothing mud bath. That always helps me."

The other animals ignored her, except for one monkey who shouted, "Just wait till you become a mother. You'll see."

"I'll be a *relaxed* mother," Taweret told him, but the monkey was already swinging to the other side of its cage, shrieking all the way.

Taweret sighed. "Now what was it you wanted to know?" she asked us.

"The baby crocodile," I said.

"The one who was in the cage next door," Miu added.

"Did you talk to him?" Khepri asked.

"Little Sobek Junior?" Taweret bobbed her huge head. "Oh, yes, I sure did. I'm not normally big on crocodiles, but he was sweet. And can you believe it? He was royalty. A crown prince. Pretty amazing, huh?"

So we were on the right track!

"Do you know where he went?" Miu asked.

Taweret chuckled. "Oh, he found a way out. With a bit of help."

"From who?" Khepri chirped.

"Why, the boy," Taweret said.

"You mean Ahmose?" I said.

"No, I mean the boy who visited before dawn," Taweret said. "I think he said his name was Dedi."

CHAPTER 17

The Fate of Two Kingdoms

I jumped onto the clay bricks that encircled Taweret's enclosure, resting my paws by the cage bars. "He called himself Dedi? Are you sure?"

"Oh, yes," Taweret said. "He said hi to Sobek Junior, and I heard him plain as plain. He was taller than the boy who lives here—"

"You mean Ahmose?" Miu asked. She had her paws up next to mine.

"Yes, Ahmose," Taweret confirmed. "This Dedi had a lighter voice, too. And he had great eyesight and balance, at least for a human. There was only the moon to see by, and he didn't trip once."

"That sounds like Dedi," I said. "He might be a prince, but he has the eyes of a cat."

"He was royal?" Taweret said in surprise. "Well, that explains why he wanted to groove with the crocodile prince. He went from cage to cage until he found him."

"And he helped the crocodile escape?" Khepri prompted.

"Oh, yes. That boy squeezed him through the bars and said he was going to take him back to the Nile. I guess he could see that Sobek Junior needed his mom and dad." She chuckled. "Of course, as soon as he got Sobek Junior out of his cage, things got more complicated."

"Complicated how?" Miu asked.

"Well, Sobek Junior was a little over-excited," Taweret said. "And when baby crocodiles get overexcited, they start nipping. They don't mean any harm by it. It's instinct."

I gaped at her, horrified. "Are you saying Sobek Junior ate Dedi?"

"Oh, he was far too small for that. But he kept snapping, and the boy was struggling to keep his mouth closed when they left here. I hope they made it to the Nile without any bad bites."

"It doesn't look like they made it there at all," I told her.

"Or if they did, something went wrong," Khepri said. "The crocodiles haven't seen Sobek Junior, and Dedi is missing, too."

"That's a real bummer." Taweret's small eyes widened. "That sweet boy, and the little crocodile—no one knows where they are?"

"Not us, anyway," Khepri said. "We're stumped."

"But I'm sure we'll figure it out," I told Taweret. "Nobody stumps the Great Detectives for long."

At least, I hoped nobody could. Truthfully, I was starting to get the teensiest bit discouraged. The sun was high in the sky, and we'd been searching for hours with no results.

"Well, I'll leave it in your capable paws, then," Taweret said. Her vast body began to quiver and shake as she retreated from us. "You know, this has been a bit intense. It's time I settled back into my mud pond."

"Our capable paws," I repeated. "Right." What would the crocodiles say when they heard that Dedi had kidnapped their crown prince and then disappeared?

"Though I do wonder," Taweret mused, "if maybe . . . No. That's just silly."

"You wonder what?" Khepri chirped.

Taweret's legs were vanishing rapidly into the mud, and her belly was following. "No, no, it really is too silly. Besides, I wouldn't want to make her life more complicated than it already is."

I poked my head through the bars of the cage. With a difficult witness, it's best to maintain eye contact. But that's a tall order when your witness is a submerging hippo. By now only Taweret's head and the ridge of her back were showing.

"What are you talking about?" I demanded. "Tell us right now, or I'll—"

Hmmmm . . . How exactly do you threaten a hippo?

"I'll . . . I'll . . . er . . ."

"Shhh, Ra," Khepri whispered in my ear. "Let Miu do the talking."

"Please, Taweret." Miu squeezed her head through the bars. "Whatever happened, we need to know about it, no matter how silly it seems. You have such a big heart—"

"Of course she does," I muttered to Khepri.

"She's a hippo. If she had a small heart, it would conk out."

"Shhh," Khepri said again.

"—and you're so sensible and responsible," Miu went on to Taweret. "I know you wouldn't want to do anything that might put two crown princes in danger."

Taweret rose slightly in the water. "You think it's that important?"

"Yes," Miu said. "I do. The fate of two kingdoms rests on your back."

"Wow." Taweret swiveled both ears as she considered this. "That's heavy, you guys."

"It's true," Miu told her.

Taweret let out a big hippo sigh. "Then I guess I'd better tell you that someone else was in the zoo that night."

"Who?" I demanded.

She hesitated. "Yaba."

What kind of answer was that? "Yeah but what?" I asked.

"She didn't say *yeah, but*," Khepri murmured in my ear. "She said *Yaba*."

I twitched my whiskers. "And who's that?"

"The other wife," Miu reminded me. "The one that Pharaoh married to seal an alliance."

"She comes here most nights," Taweret said. "She sits by the gazelle's cage, and sometimes she talks to her."

"She knows the gazelle?" Khepri said.

"Not personally," Taweret said. "But she says there are gazelles where she comes from, and she misses them. And she says she and the gazelle are like sisters because they both have to live in cages. Deep stuff like that." More cautiously, she added, "Not that I've seen Yaba's cage, mind you. She seems to walk around freely."

"So how did she get into the zoo?" Khepri asked. "Is it locked up at night?"

Taweret chuckled at the thought. "Oh, no. The gate has a simple latch, that's all. You must have seen it when you came in. It's impossible for us to open, without fingers and thumbs, but it's easy for humans like Yaba. Ahmose visits sometimes, too, and the tutor comes to fetch him. And other people visit when they can't sleep. The Keeper tells them they shouldn't, but he's a sound sleeper himself, and he's the only guard around here at night. His bunk is by the storeroom, but he snores through everything."

"So who visited the zoo last night?" Miu asked.

"Just Yaba and the boy Dedi," Taweret said.

"And Yaba was here when Dedi came?" Khepri asked.

"Yes. She was sitting by the gazelle's cage when he crept in. I don't think he even noticed she was there. But when Dedi walked away with the crocodile, she followed him out."

I sat up fast, startled. "You think she was the kidnapper?"

"Of course not." Taweret's ears twiddled worriedly. "Don't you understand what I've been telling you? Yaba is a gentle soul. She wouldn't hurt a fly. All she did was leave a minute or two after the boy. So I thought maybe she might have seen something that would help you. But she's not *guilty*."

Leaning up against my ear, Khepri clicked thoughtfully. "But—"

"Aha!" The Keeper jumped out at us. "I *knew* you cats were around here somewhere. No wonder my animals are so upset this morning." His broom flew down, headed straight for me. "Out, out, out!"

"He needs to chill," Taweret said reproachfully.

"Don't worry," I told her, dodging the broom easily. "This is playtime."

"Come on, Ra. We should go." Miu was already darting for the gate.

When I followed her, Khepri swooned as he caught a whiff of the dung pit. "Ooooooooh! Can't we stop, Ra? Just to let it soak in?"

"Some other time," I panted. "Miu's getting ahead of us." I trotted on, but before I could catch up with her, I saw something ahead that froze my fur.

It was Lady Satiah, looking angrier than ever.

CHAPTER 18

Yaba

Fortunately, Lady Satiah wasn't angry with me. Her fury was directed at the woman standing in front of her—a woman who was small and young and simply dressed. At first I thought she must be a servant. But a servant would have shrunk before Lady Satiah's wrath. This woman held her head proudly.

Lady Satiah growled like a panther. "Yaba, you lie."

So this was Yaba!

"Circle around so we can see her better," Khepri whispered.

I sidled over—and when I saw Yaba's face, I got a shock. She was the quick-witted

woman who had protected me from the lion cub. Even now, scowling at Lady Satiah, she had a certain sweetness.

As Lady Satiah stared her down, Yaba's chin went up another notch, and her scowl deepened. "I have been telling you the truth, Lady Satiah. I did not kidnap the boy. I did not harm him in any way. I did not even meet him."

"And I should trust your word?" Lady Satiah sneered. "Barbarian that you are?"

"I am no barbarian," Yaba fired back. "I am the daughter of the ruler of a great kingdom. And if my father heard you speak to me this way—"

"But he won't," Lady Satiah interrupted. "You are one of many, many daughters, and you are the child of a low-born wife. You are of no importance to him whatsoever. He sent you into exile for your whole life, merely so that he could seal a deal."

"Yikes!" Khepri whispered into my ear. "That's pretty harsh."

I nodded. It was. But it wasn't the first time I'd heard of this kind of thing. It's not much fun being a princess. At least not when you grow up.

"Unless, of course, your father gave you another mission?" Lady Satiah went on. "Perhaps he asked you to serve as an Assyrian spy."

Yaba recoiled in shock. "Don't be ridiculous!"

"It does not seem ridiculous to me," Lady Satiah said, "or to my brother." She raised a hand toward General Wegaf, who was standing, slump-shouldered, on her right.

"Or to my steward." She nodded at the portly man in the pristine tunic, standing on her left.

"It *is* ridiculous," Yaba insisted.

Ignoring her, Lady Satiah went on. "These are the facts." She ticked them off on her fingers. "One, we have searched the entire palace, top to bottom, and Ramses Dedumose is nowhere to be found. Two, the watchmen found you wandering the house last night—"

"I was sleepwalking!"

"So you say. But I have my doubts," Lady Satiah told her. "Perhaps you attacked the boy—because your father sent you here to destroy Pharaoh and his family from within."

Yaba stared at her openmouthed. "You think I'm an assassin?"

"You deny it?"

"Of course I do!" Yaba's hands balled into fists. "How dare you say such a thing? It's wicked, and it doesn't even make sense. Ask the watchmen. Hormin and Qen know I was sleepwalking. They brought me back to my room."

"I have spoken with both watchmen," Lady Satiah said. "At length. That is why I have called you here. I think they accepted your sleepwalking act too easily. They find you charming, for some strange reason. Also, they both have colds."

So that's why Hormin was sniffling and Qen had a red nose.

"They've admitted that their hearing isn't what it ought to be, and their sight is blurry, too." Lady Satiah drew closer to Yaba. "When they caught you by the gates, they thought you'd sleepwalked there from your room. But I believe you slipped past them earlier in the night, and they caught you coming back."

"Coming back from *what*?"

"You tell me." Lady Satiah regarded Yaba through narrowed eyes. "Were you meeting another spy on the landing and telling him you'd fulfilled your mission? Did you encourage the boy to go out in a dangerous boat? Or were you trying to get rid of his body?"

"This is outrageous!" Yaba spluttered. "I refuse to listen to any more of it."

As she backed away from Lady Satiah, Lady Satiah signaled to her steward. He strode forward and grabbed Yaba, pinning her arms to her sides.

"Lock her up," Lady Satiah said. "And find someone to stand guard over her. She is a danger to us all."

As the Steward dragged Yaba off, Miu came rushing into the room. "Hey, where were you guys? I thought you were right behind me."

Quickly, we filled her in on what had happened.

"What do you think?" Miu asked us. "Could Yaba be guilty?"

"At this point, we can't rule it out," Khepri said.

"No way," I insisted. "It has to be Lady Satiah."

"But Lady Satiah had the palace searched," Miu pointed out. "Why would she do that if she were guilty?"

I'd been thinking that over. "She just said she did, to throw everyone off."

"But Hormin and Qen were searching the place," Khepri said.

"On the Steward's orders," I reminded him. "Not Lady Satiah's. And she said they couldn't search the General's rooms."

"Well, she definitely had the kitchens searched," Miu told me. "When I ran out of the zoo, I saw a serving boy headed that way with a platter from Lady Satiah's breakfast, so I thought I should follow."

I perked up at the mention of breakfast. "A platter? What was on it?"

"Roast quail, maybe? I wasn't paying attention. Not after that yummy fish snack I had. Plus, I was trying make sure no one noticed me."

I politely ignored the mention of fish. "Roast quail? That's one of my favorites. Was there any sauce on it?"

"I told you, I don't remember," Miu said, sounding a touch exasperated. "What I'm trying to say is that there was a search party in the kitchens, and they said they were there on Lady Satiah's orders. So she did give that command."

"Maybe they were only pretending to

 152

search," I said. "Tell you what—I'll go search the kitchen myself." I licked my chops, thinking of that leftover quail.

"They've already inspected it from top to bottom," Miu said. "And so have I. Dedi isn't there, and neither is Sobek Junior."

I have to admit, I was a bit disappointed to hear that—and not only because she hadn't found Dedi. I sat back on my haunches. "Well, maybe Lady Satiah had the kitchens searched because she knew Dedi wasn't there," I said. "She's got him locked up somewhere else."

"Or maybe she's innocent, Ra." Khepri hopped from my head to the floor, tapping the tiles for emphasis. "That's the simplest explanation."

"Remember what she said to General Wegaf?" I reminded him. "About her plan, and how she was going to deal with Dedi?"

"That didn't sound good," Khepri admitted. "But if she's guilty, why is she trying to get a confession from Yaba?"

"It's a bluff," I said. "She's trying to cover up her own guilt by accusing Yaba."

"I guess that's possible," Miu said slowly.

"But there are good reasons to suspect Yaba, too. The watchmen do have colds, and they might have missed her—especially if it turns out she's a trained spy."

"Over at the stables, they say that relations between Pharaoh and the Assyrians are rocky," Khepri mused.

"Oh, they're always rocky," I said.

"All the more reason why an Assyrian ruler might want to hurt Pharaoh and his family," Miu said. "I don't think we can rule Yaba out."

"But I liked her," I protested. "She was nice to me. She saved me from that lion cub. Remember, Khepri?"

"Of course I remember." Khepri's antennae shivered. "I was right there. And I had a close-up view of those teeth. But being kind to cats doesn't make her innocent."

"It should," I grumbled.

"Ra, be reasonable," Miu chided.

"It's reasonable to trust my instincts," I told her. "And my Great Detective instincts say it isn't Yaba."

Miu looked unimpressed. "Great Detectives also look at the facts, Ra."

"And it's a fact that Yaba is lying," Khepri said.

"What are you talking about?" I said.

Khepri's reedy voice was sure. "Yaba said she was sleepwalking when the watchmen saw her. But we know she wasn't. She'd been visiting the zoo, remember? And she followed Dedi out."

"Maybe she was sleepwalking the whole time," I mumbled. But now I was starting to have my doubts. What if Yaba was guilty?

There was only one way to tell for sure.

"I'm going to get her to talk," I told Khepri and Miu.

CHAPTER 19

Brainpower

Cats are like gods in Egypt, but I'll admit our reputation might be a teensy bit overblown. We can't cure diseases or protect women in childbirth or vanquish evil spirits, the way the cat goddess Bastet can. Yet we flesh-and-blood cats do have some magic in us, a magic that even the tiniest tabby kitten possesses. When we purr, we can make humans talk.

It's a magic that works best on our own family. With strangers, we might only get a "Nice kitty." Not exactly the kind of information you can use to crack a case.

Still, it seemed worth a try.

"Climb aboard," I told Khepri. "Let's go find Yaba."

With a sigh, Khepri hopped on. "I don't think this is going to work, Ra."

"Of course it will," I said. "It's a brilliant idea." I headed off in the direction that the Steward had dragged Yaba.

Miu came with me, but she had her doubts, too. "Ra, we don't even know her."

"She's married to Pharaoh," I said, "so that makes her family."

"I'm not sure a diplomatic marriage counts." Miu trailed behind me. "Even Pharaoh hardly knows her. It's not what I'd call a strong family tie."

"And she'll be locked up," Khepri reminded me. "How are you going to get in to purr to her?"

"I'll think of something." Pharaoh's Cat is nothing if not resourceful. I bounded forward with confidence.

I lost my bounce, however, when we found the Steward in front of a stout wooden door. He was giving orders to Hormin and Qen.

"I don't care what Yaba says," the Steward insisted. "Don't let her out. If you do, you're fired."

Hormin bent his head and sniffled. "Yes, my lord Steward. We understand."

"She's sneaky," the Steward warned. "Don't let her fool you. And don't let anyone in."

Qen looked like he was about to complain, but Hormin elbowed him and said, "We won't, my lord."

As the Steward hurried away, Qen hissed, "Why'd you let him saddle us with another job, Hormin? We haven't had a break since yesterday night."

"You don't say no to the Steward," Hormin told him. "Besides, he said he'd send someone to take over from us soon. We won't be here long."

"Want to bet?" Qen slumped against the doorframe, his nose redder than ever. "I have to tell you, Hormin, I'm having second thoughts about working here. I know you say it's worth it, but—"

"Stop being such a big crybaby," Hormin snapped. "We're guarding a spoiled princess, okay? It's not a big deal."

"That's another thing," Qen said. "Yaba isn't spoiled. She's nice. She always smiles at us. I don't like that they're locking her up."

"I can't believe you're defending her," Hormin said. "She made fools of us with that sleepwalking act. And here you are, sweet on her, like she's your girlfriend or something."

Qen's whole face was bright red now. "I'm not sweet on her. I just said she smiles a lot. Anyway, it's not like she's the only one who was wandering around last night. Remember that noise we heard near Lady Satiah's room?"

"And you think we'll keep our jobs if we mention that?" Hormin shook his head. "No,

Qen. You go making accusations against Lady Satiah, and she'll feed us to the crocodiles."

"Hey, that's more evidence against Lady Satiah," I whispered to Khepri.

"Maybe," was all Khepri said.

As Hormin and Qen continued to bicker, I stared at the door behind them. The wood was so thick you could barely hear Yaba shouting, "Let me out!" Even worse, the door had two hefty bolts locking it shut, far too high for any cat to reach. When I sauntered up for a closer look, Hormin stomped hard, almost squashing my tail.

"Scat!" Qen growled.

"Yeowch!" I retreated toward Miu.

"Keep going," Khepri whispered in my ear. "They're still staring at you."

Miu nudged me along. "We're never going to get in there, Ra. And even if we did, Yaba might not talk to you. We'll have to solve this case some other way."

I hated to admit it, but she was probably right. As we walked away from Hormin and Qen, I thought hard, and soon I had an even better plan.

"Okay," I said. "Here's what we'll do. We'll follow Lady Satiah's every step. She'll have to go to Dedi at some point. And when she does, we'll catch her in the act."

It was a great idea, one of my best. But Miu and Khepri couldn't appreciate just how clever it was.

"But what if she isn't guilty, Ra?" Miu said. "We'll have wasted a whole day while the real criminal gets away."

"And even if she is guilty," Khepri added, "she might not deal with Dedi herself. She could give the dirty work to someone else, the way she made the Steward lock up Yaba. And we wouldn't miss it."

Okay, so maybe my idea wasn't quite so great as I thought.

Discouraged, I stalked through the nearest arched doorway. It opened onto a neglected garden guarded by a grubby statue of ibis-headed Thoth, god of wisdom. Gazing around, I thought of Pharaoh, walking in his gardens. Pharaoh, who had asked me to guard his children.

"Well, then you come up with an idea," I told Miu and Khepri. "Because we have to do *something*. Dedi is missing. He's in danger. We can't turn our backs on him."

Khepri kneaded my fur impatiently. "No one's asking you to turn your back on anyone, Ra. I'm just saying that we need to stop dashing around without a proper plan."

"I agree," Miu said, coming up beside me.

"Brainpower," Khepri said, still kneading my fur. "That's what will solve this mystery."

"You think I'm not using my brain already?" I was upset. "Khepri, I'm using everything I've got. Heart, nose, paws, head. I've been working so hard I haven't even had breakfast. But it's no use. Dedi is lost."

Was Dedi locked away somewhere like Yaba? Was he scared? In pain? I'd managed to push that thought away for most of the day, but I couldn't any longer.

"What if we don't get to him in time?" I shivered. "Pharaoh will never forgive me. I don't think I could forgive myself. I mean, I know I sometimes call Pharaoh's kids annoying, but they're my family. I've known Dedi since he was a baby. I'd do anything to keep him safe. I . . . I . . ."

Something strange was happening to me. Normally, I find it quite easy to talk about my family. But my throat was suddenly tight.

Miu brushed against me. "Oh, Ra. Of course we know you love Pharaoh's children. And we're going to find Dedi. I'm sure of it."

Khepri peered down over my brow, his beady eyes contrite. "I'm sorry, Ra. I wasn't trying to criticize you. I just meant we should take a few minutes to look at things logically. Let's draw up a list of suspects. Lady Satiah is one, and so is Yaba, but I'm sure there are more."

I took a deep breath. "Okay. I guess we could do that."

"First, we need to look at opportunity," Khepri went on. "Who had a chance to attack Dedi?"

I considered this. "Well, there aren't many watchmen here, so I'd say pretty much everybody in the palace had a chance."

"Except for the kitchen staff and most of the servants," Miu said. "They're locked into their own wing of the palace for the night. I heard them talking about it when I was inspecting the kitchens."

"And you're sure they couldn't get out?" Khepri asked her.

"You bet they can't," came a kooky whistle above me. "Oop-oop."

Who Benefits?

Even before I looked up, I knew who it was. So did Khepri, who was already sliding down to my belly fur.

"Where have you been?" I said to Hoop.

"I had things to do," Hoop said cheerfully. "Feathers to preen, bugs to catch . . ."

At the mention of bugs, Khepri quivered against my belly.

"Quit scaring the beetle," I said.

"That's right." Miu backed me up. "Leave our friend alone."

"Did I touch him?" Hoop said indignantly. "Did I even get close?" He winked at us. "Though he'd make quite a meal. You could feed a family and still have leftovers."

I swiped at him with my paw, but he only hopped back, laughing hard.

"Tell your friend he's safe with me. Oop-oop! I don't eat bugs I've been introduced to. It wouldn't be polite."

Khepri crept a little way out from my belly and whispered, "Ask him about the servants."

I looked down at him, confused. The servants?

Miu worked it out. "So what I heard in the kitchens is right?" she asked Hoop. "The servants can't get out at night?"

"Nope. That wing's locked off every night, tight as an unhatched egg. Lady Satiah doesn't want anyone stealing from her."

"So who doesn't get locked up?" I asked.

Hoop tilted his head so that the light caught his copper head feathers. "Well, Lady Satiah, for one. And the Painter of Her Mouth. She sleeps outside Lady Satiah's door."

"So she'd notice if Lady Satiah left her room?" Khepri asked, growing bolder.

"The Painter? Don't you believe it. Nothing would wake that lady. Snores like a wild boar."

 166

"Who else is able to move around at night?" Miu asked.

Hoop thought about it some more. "The Steward. And Hormin and Qen. Oh, and Ahmose, of course. And Turo the tutor. And the Keeper of the Zoo. And Yaba. And General Wegaf, while he's visiting." He snapped at a gnat in the air. "Hey, why are you asking all these questions, anyway?"

"We're Great Detectives," I told him, "and we're trying to solve a crime. The kidnapping of Pharaoh's son."

"And the disappearance of a crocodile prince," Miu added.

Hoop whistled. "You don't say? Oop-oop!"

"You didn't see them, did you?" I asked. "They were together, the boy and the crocodile, just before dawn—"

"Just before dawn?" Hoop laughed. "Are you kidding? I'm busy then."

"With what?" Miu asked.

"Why, bringing the sun up, what do you think? Night would never end if it weren't for us hoopoes." As we stared up at him, he executed a neat bow. "You're too awed to speak, I see. Never mind. You can thank me later."

"Actually, we'd rather ask you more questions," Khepri said.

"It'll have to wait. Gotta get to my favorite lunch spot before someone else does. Catch you later!" Hoop took off for a high ridge at the far end of the garden, where he shoved his beak into the wall, searching for bugs.

The mention of lunch did not improve my temper.

"Some help he is," I fumed.

"Actually, he was a help," Miu said happily. "We have a complete list of suspects now: Lady Satiah. The Painter of Her Mouth. The Steward. Hormin and Qen. The Keeper of the Zoo. The General. Ahmose. The tutor. And Yaba."

"Any of them could have done it," Khepri agreed, crawling out into full view.

"But that's ten people," I said, aghast. "We can't follow all ten." I frowned at the distant hoopoe, who was slurping up his lunch with great enjoyment. "And Hoop knows it, too. I bet he did it himself, and he's lying to us to cover up his tracks."

Miu blinked. "Don't be silly, Ra."

"Why on earth would a hoopoe kidnap a prince?" Khepri asked me. "Besides, he's not big enough to do the job. I think we're after a human here."

"Ten of them," I moaned.

"For now," Khepri said. "But if we think about motives, we can narrow the field down."

"Motives?" I repeated. "You mean, why someone might have committed the crime?"

"Precisely," Khepri confirmed. "Let's take the Keeper, for instance."

"Well, that's easy," I said. "He would do it because he's a horrible person who chucks brooms at cats."

Khepri and Miu looked at each other. For some reason, they both sighed.

"That's not much of a motive, Ra," Miu said. "Especially since the only reason he went after you with a broom was to protect the animals in his zoo."

"Well, maybe he saw Dedi stealing the crocodile and he was overcome with rage," I said.

"I don't think he would hurt Pharaoh's son," Miu said. "And anyway, he would have put the crocodile back in his cage. Which we know he didn't."

"But—"

"Ra, listen," Khepri said. "The question we have to ask is this: Who benefits if Dedi disappears?"

Who benefits? Hmmmm . . .

"Lady Satiah," I said. "Because her son is closer to the throne."

"And Yaba," Miu said. "If she is working as a spy for her father."

"Who else?" Khepri said. "Let's go through the list."

We couldn't think of a way that the Painter benefited, or the Steward, or the watchmen.

"Ahmose benefits," Miu said. "He would

become Pharaoh's oldest son. And if Pharaoh thought Dedi ran away of his own accord, he wouldn't be angry with Ahmose. He might even decide to make him his heir one day. But Ahmose seems like a nice kid. I can't believe he would do such a thing."

"I can't, either," Khepri said. "Unless he was upset about Dedi trying to put his crocodile back in the Nile—"

"No," I said firmly. "It's like the Keeper of the Zoo. Ahmose would have grabbed the crocodile and put him back in the zoo."

"And he was surprised to hear the crocodile was missing, remember?" Miu said. "He wanted the Keeper to tell his mother about it."

Khepri paced around the edge of the garden, thinking hard. "What about Ahmose's tutor, Turo? If Ahmose became Pharaoh's heir, Turo would become a much more important person. He'd be the prince's tutor and his cousin, and he'd have lots of influence."

"He didn't encourage the Keeper to report the missing crocodile," Miu recalled.

"And remember how he kept yawning

this morning?" Khepri said. "He was short on sleep. So maybe he was up before dawn, going after Dedi."

"Khepri, I think you're onto something," Miu said, excited. "We should—"

"Shhh!" I flattened myself against the statue of Thoth. "Someone's coming."

Two someones, in fact. First the Painter of Her Mouth arrived, her tiny sandals beating pitter-pat on the mud-brick garden path as she dashed behind a bush. Then came the Steward, eyes darting this way and that, until he spied the fluttering edge of the Painter's tunic and went after her.

"Uh-oh." Khepri scrambled back up to my head for a better view. "Did she upset Lady Satiah? Is that why he's after her?"

We waited to find out, but there was no yelling, only whispers.

"They're up to something," Miu said.

We crept closer and peered through the bush.

The Steward and the Painter were kissing!

"Ick," Khepri clicked.

"Eww," I agreed.

"Shhh!" said Miu.

The Steward didn't seem to care that his beautiful tunic was getting crumpled. "My darling!" he whispered. "You've been so brave, so resourceful. You've made everything possible."

"I did it for you," the Painter whispered back. "For us. We need a fresh start."

"I must go," he said. "But tonight we will make our move."

"And then we will be together forever," she breathed.

He kissed her again.

"Ick," Khepri clicked.

"Eww," I agreed.

"Shhh!" said Miu. "Did you see what she gave him?"

I hadn't. Khepri had missed it, too. And now the Steward was walking away.

"A linen bag!" Miu told us. "And it clinked. I'll bet you anything that Dedi's jewelry is in it. Look! He's stuffed it down his tunic."

We saw the bulge above the Steward's sash.

"Why, those rotten, no-good thieves!" I bristled as the Painter pattered past us. "How dare they steal Dedi's things!"

Khepri rucked up the fur between my ears, the way he did when was thinking hard. "They might be more than thieves."

Miu swished her tail. "What do you mean?"

"Well, it sounds like they've been desperate to start a new life together, but they didn't have the funds for it. Then they saw Dedi's jewelry. Ordinarily, they wouldn't dare touch it. The punishment for stealing royal gold is a harsh one. Who wants to lose a hand or a nose? But if they made it look like Dedi ran off with his own jewelry, they could get away with it."

We all looked down at the ground, where the faint, small marks of the Painter's sandals could be seen.

Miu gasped. "They're like the ones on the landing, between the palace and the river. The ones that were supposed to be Dedi's."

"Those monsters!" I started after them. "They won't get away with it!"

Khepri tugged at my fur, trying to hold me in check. "Ra, we don't know that they're guilty. It's one possibility."

"It's the right one," I told him as we reached the cool, polished floors of the palace again. "My instincts are telling me so."

"The same way they told you Lady Satiah was guilty?" Miu asked.

"Maybe she's in it, too," I said. "Maybe they're all guilty. Maybe it's a conspiracy!"

"Ra, that doesn't make any sense," Khepri said.

"It sure doesn't," Miu agreed.

"It does to me. And I'm going to get them." I sniffed around for the Steward's footprints. I was going to claw that bag away from him if it was the last thing I did. "Just you wait and—"

I stopped. I'd picked up the scent of someone very familiar. It wasn't the Steward, or the Painter, or Lady Satiah. It was someone I knew much, much better. Someone who couldn't possibly be here . . .

I dashed over to a large trunk painted with vultures and crocodiles.

"Ra, what are you doing?" Khepri asked.

"I don't believe it," Miu said behind me.

We peered over the trunk—and found Kiya.

CHAPTER 21

Kidnapped

Kiya was well hidden behind the trunk, but she didn't look happy. Her cheeks were tearstained, her hair was tangled, and she smelled like rotten meat. But her round face beamed with delight when she saw me.

"Ra-baby!"

She put her arms around me, and I didn't even try to resist. I purred and purred and purred—and not only because I wanted her to talk.

"Oh, Ra-baby!" she murmured, snuggling me close. "I couldn't go home. I just couldn't. Dedi's *here*, and I have to find him. You understand, don't you?"

"Purr some more," Khepri urged.

While Miu stood guard at the corner of the trunk, I purred even more loudly, until Kiya giggled.

"You should have seen my bed on the boat," she said. "I told Nurse I wanted to rest, and I pulled the curtains shut so it looked like I was sleeping. Then I sneaked out and climbed in the meat crate that the cook didn't want. After they carried it back inside the palace, all I had to do was climb out when no one was looking."

I was impressed. And horrified.

"Doesn't she realize the danger she's in?" Miu whispered, echoing my own thoughts. "Whoever went after Dedi might go after her, too."

Sandals flapped nearby. Kiya froze.

So she knew she had to be careful. That was something.

As the sandal slaps died away, we relaxed.

"Are you hungry, Ra-baby?" Kiya whispered. "I'm hungry, too. Let's sneak into the kitchens and get some snacks."

Snacks? I was tempted.

"No, Ra," Miu warned. "It would put her in terrible danger."

"No snacks," Khepri agreed.

"That's easy for you to say." I hopped out of Kiya's lap. "You've eaten. But Kiya and I haven't. And if I don't take her to go get snacks, she'll probably go on her own—"

"Okay, Ra-baby," Kiya whispered. "Let's go now."

"No!" Miu tried to pull her back.

Kiya was so strong, she didn't even notice. She crept out from behind the trunk—just as Turo the tutor appeared in the doorway.

"Pharaoh's daughter?" He stared at her, astonished. Then he dived for her and slipped a hand over her mouth. Swinging her off her feet, he carried her away.

We followed them, of course—meowing fit to bust and scratching at Turo's legs. Nothing made him let go of Kiya. He dragged her through two empty rooms, then shut the door on us.

We clawed at the door, but it was no use. Even Khepri couldn't get through the gap underneath.

"I can't hear anything," he reported. "Not even footsteps. Maybe there's more than one room?"

I was in a panic. "Where is she? What's he doing to her? How do we get to her?"

I meowed loudly, hoping a human would come to help. But the only answer I got came from a window high above us, and there wasn't anything human or helpful about it.

"How's the case going?" Nekhbet the vulture leered down at us. "Found little Sobek Junior yet?"

We gaped up at her.

"The crocodiles are waiting, you know," she clacked self-importantly. "And they're not the patient type."

"Well, they're going to have to be," Miu said. "We have other things on our minds right now."

"I see." Annoyed, Nekhbet picked at the window ledge with her talons. "Well, I was going to tell you what we've discovered, but it will have to wait. I can't stick around here, not with Lady Satiah ordering her servants to shoot at vultures. I only came because it was so important."

"What's important?" Miu called out.

But Nekhbet had already flapped her wings and gone.

"What if it's about the boat?" I said, worried. "Maybe the crocodiles found it, with Dedi in it. Or he used to be in it, and now he's not. Or maybe they were lying to us before. Maybe"—my heart pounded—"they're holding him hostage."

"We've got to go talk to them," Miu said.

"But then they'll know we don't have little Sobek Junior," Khepri chirped anxiously.

"And what about Kiya?" I said, turning back to the door.

"You two stay here and try to get to her," Miu said. "I'll deal with the crocodiles." Her mottled fur rose in anger. "If they've hurt Dedi, I'll let them have it."

"No!" Khepri and I spoke at exactly the same time.

Miu confronting the crocodiles? Not a good idea. Especially not if they might be holding Dedi hostage.

"Miu, we need you to work on getting to Kiya," Khepri said. "There might be a window somewhere, and you're the best climber we've got."

I drew myself up. "Khepri, I'm a fine climber, and you know it—"

"We're headed to the crocodiles, Ra." Khepri raced to the top of my head. "We've got to save Dedi, if we can."

CHAPTER 22

Another Crocodile

With Khepri perched between my ears, I zoomed through the palace, determined to get the truth out of the crocodiles. But when we reached the gates that led to the river landing, they were closed. Lady Satiah, Ahmose, and the Keeper of the Zoo were standing in front of them.

Trembling, the Keeper bowed low before Lady Satiah. "I'm sorry, my lady. One of the lion cubs won't take any food, and he's not drinking much, either. He may not make it through the night."

"You mean I'm going to lose another animal?" Lady Satiah jerked at her wig, enraged. "Just what do you think you're running, Keeper—a zoo or a tomb?"

"A zoo, my lady," the Keeper quavered. "The very best zoo I know how to run. But I can't work miracles. Sometimes animals get sick. Especially if they're overcrowded—"

"Those animals are eating me out of house and home," Lady Satiah snarled. "And you want me to build an even bigger zoo? No, Keeper. Those animals are here to serve my purposes. I am not here to serve them."

As Ahmose bit his lip, I murmured to Khepri, "Her purposes? What is she talking about?"

"Isn't it obvious?" Khepri said.

It wasn't. But I wasn't about to admit that.

"You'll get no more money from me," Lady Satiah told the Keeper. "Find some other way to keep those animals alive."

The Keeper's wrinkles deepened. "My lady, I will do what I can for the cub, and perhaps he will live." His voice shook. "But I must also tell you that the baby crocodile has gone missing. I think he escaped back into the Nile."

Lady Satiah glared at him. "Then get me another one. They're all the same, anyway. No one will care."

The Keeper winced. "My lady, I am not strong enough—"

"Then find someone else to do it." Her bracelets jingled as she jabbed a finger at him. "Just get me a crocodile. Now!"

"Yes, my lady." The Keeper scuttled toward the door.

Ahmose watched in envy. "Mother, can I help him? Please?"

"No, Ahmose." She pulled him close. "Pharaoh is coming soon, and we must be prepared." She smoothed his hair with restless fingers. "You know what to do."

"Yes, Mother." With a quick, miserable glance at Lady Satiah, he added, "But won't Pharaoh be angry when he finds out about Dedi?"

"I will handle it," Lady Satiah told him.

"But what if he blames us?"

"Do not concern yourself about that," Lady Satiah said. "You are Pharaoh's son, and such worries are beneath you. Remember, all things are possible—if you play your part well. And then Pharaoh won't neglect you anymore." She tweaked a stray lock of his hair.

Ahmose flinched.

Behind them, the Keeper pushed open the gates to the landing.

"Quick, Ra!" Khepri whispered. "To the crocodiles!"

I dashed after the Keeper and followed him out.

On the landing itself, all was chaos. The floodwaters had swallowed the lower piers, and workmen were hauling barrels and small boats out of the river's reach. Other men were repairing a damaged gangplank. Armed with spears, Hormin and Qen stood guard against the many crocodiles swimming dangerously close.

"Get me one little baby crocodile," the Keeper begged Hormin and Qen. "I'll find you a net."

"Not on your life," Hormin sniffled.

"Yeah," Qen agreed. "There's a limit to what we'll do for you."

"Keep your mind on the job," Hormin warned Qen. "Don't let him distract you."

"I only need a small one." The Keeper pointed at an enormous crocodile, lying in wait in the floodwaters. "Smaller than that one's snout."

The crocodile lunged upward, aiming at the Keeper.

"Watch out!" Hormin hauled the Keeper out of danger. "You nearly lost your foot there. Didn't you see him coming?"

Shaking, the Keeper knelt down and touched his toes, as if checking to make sure they were all there. "I . . . I didn't think he'd attack me. Animals usually sense I'm their friend."

"You lousy kidnapper!" the crocodile roared. "Come out here and fight. I'll bite both your feet off!"

Khepri and I recognized the crocodile at the same moment he recognized us.

"It's the Admiral!" Khepri exclaimed.

I leaped to the top of the nearest wall so I could see his scaly head better. He looked faster in the water than he had on the mud-bank, and more dangerous, too.

"Where's our prince?" the Admiral snapped at me.

"Where's ours?" I countered.

"You first." The Admiral's heavy tail churned the waters.

I stood my ground. "No, you."

"Tell me what you know, or you'll regret it!" the Admiral growled. "I'm getting very hungry . . ."

Did that mean he was holding Dedi hostage?

"Er . . ." I stalled, hoping Khepri would come to my rescue.

Tipping forward to advise me, Khepri lost his balance. "Raaaaaaaaaaaa!" he cried. "Heeeeeeeeeeeeeeeelp!"

I flung a paw out to stop him, but it was too late.

Khepri hurtled toward the raging floodwaters—and the Admiral's open mouth.

CHAPTER 23

Plan B

You've probably noticed that cats are geniuses at falling. Pharaoh's Cat, in particular. I twist in the air. I turn somersaults. And I always land on my feet. (Well, almost always.)

Beetles are not geniuses. They tend to land on their backs. Fortunately, Khepri had picked up a few tricks from me. Sailing through the air, he did a double somersault and a backflip, and he landed behind the Admiral's left eye.

"Ugh! It's a bug! Get off me, you dung-eater! The Admiral tried to shake Khepri loose, but my friend clung to his scaly skin.

"Attaboy!" I called out. "Hang in there, buddy!"

The Admiral stopped twisting. *Battle won*, I thought. But then I got a good look at his cold, golden-green eyes.

"Tell me everything you know about Sobek Junior," the Admiral ordered me. "Or I'll submerge."

Khepri gasped. Some beetles are excellent swimmers, I've been told. Not Khepri.

"I'm sinking," the crocodile warned. His tail vanished under the floodwaters, and then most of his spine did, too.

"Raaaaaaaaaaa!" Khepri wailed.

"This is it." The Admiral hovered just above the waterline. "Talk, or the beetle gets it!"

"Okay, okay," I said. "I'll tell you everything I know. The princes were together, just before dawn. We know that. And our prince took your prince out of his cage—"

"Your prince stole our prince?" The Admiral raised his head, enraged.

"He didn't steal him," I explained. "He was trying to help him—"

The Admiral wasn't listening. "Okay, that does it!" he shouted, so loudly that every crocodile on the river could hear him. "It's time for Plan B."

Khepri's chirp was so high it was almost a squeak. "Plan B?"

"Plan Break-in!" the Admiral roared. As dozens of crocodiles dived deep underwater, he lunged for the landing, then fell back with a huge splash, soaking me.

"Khepri!" I shrieked.

"Right here!" My buddy flung himself onto me. "I made the leap just in time."

Surfacing, the Admiral let out a bellow that sounded like a battle cry. Every remaining crocodile on the water turned toward him, echoing the call. The Nile itself seemed to shudder, and I could have sworn that the floodwaters rose higher.

As Khepri and I watched in horror, the crocodiles surged toward the landing, hurling their bodies halfway out of the water, pale bellies twisting. The floodwaters were so high that they didn't have far to jump, and two of them made it. Jaws wide, they padded toward the terrified humans.

Qen threw his spear, but it fell short.

Holding tight to his, Hormin shouted, "Run for your lives!"

The screaming workmen didn't need to

be told. The ones repairing the gangplank
let it go. When it fell halfway into the water,
more crocodiles raced up it, including the
Admiral, who called out orders. "Take back
the palace—and find our prince!"

"Let's get out of here, Ra!" Khepri panted.

Easier said than done. All around me,
people were shrieking and stumbling over
one another. I saw Qen fall near the water's
edge.

I tried to snake through the panicked
feet of the crowd, but it was impossible.
"We'll never get out of here alive!" I wailed.

And then, above the uproar, I heard Pharaoh.

At first I thought it must be a dream. But when I leaped up onto a stack of barrels, I saw a royal barge coming down the Nile. Standing tall at the prow was Pharaoh, his face as fierce as Horus, the falcon god.

"Pharaoh's here?" I gasped. "Already?"

"But how—?" Khepri wondered aloud.

"Shhh!" I said. "He's calling my name."

"Ra," Pharaoh shouted, "where are my children?"

I'd never felt like such a failure. I almost wished the crocodiles would eat me. Dedi was still missing, and Kiya—

Kiya. I had to protect her. I shot toward the palace, bouncing across the heads of the tight-packed servants struggling to get to safety.

"Ra, where are you going?" Pharaoh shouted.

I couldn't stop. Kiya was the only thought on my mind. I reached the front of the crowd and leaped through the palace gates, just before they swung shut behind me.

"Why are they closing the gates?" Khepri said, upset. "Don't they realize they're leaving a lot of people out there? The crocodiles will get them."

"Lock the gates, men!" Inside the entranceway, General Wegaf was standing tall again, and there was a ruthless look in his eye. "Keep those crocodiles out!"

"But my brother is outside!" a young servant cried, turning to Lady Satiah. "Please, my lady—"

"Be silent!" Lady Satiah's lips were pale under their dots of red paint. "I have a son to protect."

"My lady, have you heard about Pharaoh's barge?" the Steward put in anxiously. "The watchman Hormin saw it coming down the Nile."

Hormin was sniffling more than usual. "It's true, my lady. I—"

"Pharaoh will be safe if he stays on the barge," Lady Satiah interrupted. "Anyway, he has spearmen to protect him. I expect everyone to follow General Wegaf's orders, and keep those gates closed!" In her beaded finery, she wobbled toward the General. "Brother, have you seen Ahmose?"

"The silly boy ran off," the General told her. "Not much of a soldier, is he? Need to fix that."

"Ran where?" Lady Satiah demanded, her voice trembling. "Not outside?"

"No." The General waved toward the living quarters. "Back there somewhere."

Lady Satiah hobbled off, calling, "Ahmose, where are you? Answer me right now!"

As she vanished from sight, Miu darted toward us, her eyes wide. "Kiya's disappeared! I finally found a way into the room where she was, but she's gotten out somehow. I've been looking for her everywhere."

"Kiya's gone?" I was starting to feel panicky. To lose one of Pharaoh's children was bad enough, but *both*? "I should have stayed with her. I should have kept her safe—"

"You couldn't be in two places at once, Ra," Khepri said. "Miu, is there anywhere you haven't searched yet?"

"The zoo," Miu said.

"That's where we'll go, then," Khepri said firmly. "As fast as we can!"

I ran as if the crocodiles were behind me, though thankfully they weren't. "Maybe Pharaoh's spearmen fought them off," I panted to Khepri as we neared the dung pit.

"Some of them, anyway," Khepri said. "Remember the ones who dived down? I'm a little worried about that. I have a theory—"

"What's that sound?" Miu interrupted.

Thump, thump, *thump*. I heard it, too.

Miu ran faster. "I can feel it through my paws."

I picked up speed, too. "And it's getting louder and louder."

"That would be evidence for my theory," Khepri said, but he didn't sound happy about it. "You see—"

"Is that Kiya?" I cut in. Up ahead, a small figure near the dung pit turned toward the zoo.

I shot ahead. By the time I reached the zoo archway, she was gone, but the gate to the zoo was open. I slipped through it.

Miu followed me. "Do you think she's hiding here?"

"Must be," I said. "I'll track her down by scent. I'm good at that." And it's true, I am. Most of the time. But not when a stinky dung pit has knocked out my nose.

"I can barely smell anything," I finally had to admit.

"I can't, either," Miu told me. "We'll have to ask if anyone's seen her."

I glanced around at the cages. "Well, at least we've got lots of witnesses." I turned toward the closest ones, the ibis and the lioness. "Hello again! We're looking for a girl who—"

"They stole my baby!" the lioness wailed to me. "They *stole* him. And I'll never see him again."

"Serves you right!" the ibis screamed at her. "Your cubs ate my babies."

"I'm sorry, but I'm on important business here," I told them. "If you could answer the question—"

"You don't understand," the lioness moaned. "They stole him. They stole my baby. They took him to the storeroom an hour ago. When the babies go there, they never come back."

"They're just looking after him," Miu said gently. "He's sick."

"They *stole* him," the lioness insisted. "They stole my baby."

I rolled my eyes. "Look, nobody would steal your baby, lady. I mean, what use is a lion cub to anyone?"

The lioness swung her head around to me, and her claws sprang out. I was so close to the bars that she nearly took off my nose.

"Er . . . except to his mother, of course," I babbled, backing away. "Useful thing, kids. That's why I'm looking for one. Er, not mine, that is. Pharaoh's daughter. Actually, I'm still looking for Pharaoh's son, too. And the baby crocodile. Did I mention that I'm Pharaoh's Cat?"

"I don't care whose cat you are," the lioness roared. "If you come any closer, you're dead meat!"

Up by my ears, Khepri had been chittering away to himself. Now his legs hit my fur with a bounce. "That's it! You've cracked the case, Ra!"

"I have?" I said. "Er . . . I mean . . . yes, I have. Of course."

"I can't believe I didn't see it myself," Khepri went on.

"That's all right," I told him. "Nobody cracks cases like me."

I was about to ask how I'd cracked this one, but Khepri was shouting excitedly to Miu, "Now we know what happened to Dedi!"

"We do?" Miu said.

"Lead us out of here, Ra," Khepri said to me. "We need to move now, before it's too late."

"But what about Kiya?" Miu asked.

"Dedi's in more danger right now," Khepri said. "Come on!"

I raced out of the zoo, not sure where we were going. But the moment we came out of the gate, I got a sinking feeling that I knew where Khepri was taking us. Make that a *stinking* feeling . . .

"Not the dung pit!" I gasped.

Thump, thump, THUMP. The sound was coming from deep inside the pit. And then it stopped, and there was a horrible gurgle.

"Uh-oh!" Khepri clutched my ear. "That's what I was afraid of."

"Dedi!" I flew at the pit cover, shouting his name. "Dedi, are you in there?"

"No!" Khepri cried. "Get back, Ra!"

CRUNCH! The pit cover splintered, then shattered.

I froze. The most humongous crocodile I'd ever seen was slithering out of the dung pit.

CHAPTER 24

Crunch

Within seconds, the crocodile had me trapped, his teeth snapping at my tail.

"WHERE IS MY SON?" he roared.

"Er . . . let me guess," I said weakly. "You're King Sobek, right? I'm Pharaoh's Cat. Pleased to meet you."

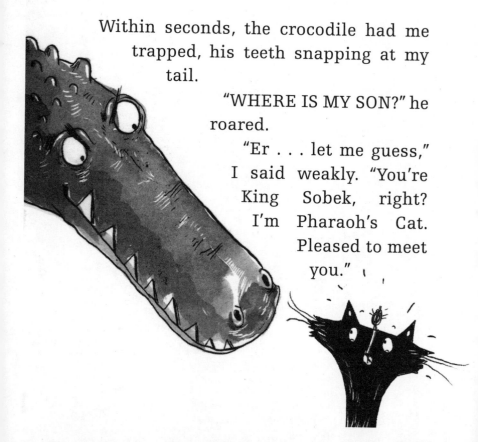

Behind him, a second enormous croco-dile slithered up from the pit. This one was female. The sight made me woozy. Or maybe that was the smell of the dung that coated her scales.

"And your lovely wife," I added. "What an unexpected treat."

"Not so unexpected," Khepri muttered. "That dung pit must empty into the Nile, and I bet it has an underwater grate to block the way into the palace. That thump-ing sound we heard was the crocodiles breaking down the grate."

The two crocodiles bared their teeth, roaring so loudly that my fur shook. "WHERE IS OUR SON?"

"Tell them, Ra!" Khepri whispered in my ear.

I couldn't tell them what I didn't know. "No, you."

"But you're the one who figured it out."

"You can give me the credit, okay?" I told him.

"But your voice is louder."

The crocodiles narrowed their eyes. Their tails began to thrash.

"Khepri, just tell them!"

"Ahem!" Khepri clicked to get their attention. "It's me, Khepri the Great Detective. Your baby is behind the door!"

"WHAT DOOR?" the king crocodile growled, tail still thrashing.

Khepri pointed. "The storeroom door."

The storeroom? But I'd been in there already, playing tag with the Keeper, and I hadn't seen a crocodile baby there. Then it hit me: Khepri was fooling the crocodiles so we could get away.

It worked. The crocodiles abandoned us for the door.

As I darted back to Miu, King Sobek slid his lower jaw into the gap at the bottom of the door, and . . .

CRUNCH!

Within seconds, the crocodiles were inside, tearing their way through the storeroom.

Crunch, crunch, crunch!

"Good job, Khepri," I said. "Let's get away now."

"No! We need to follow them," Khepri urged me.

I couldn't believe my ears. "What?"

Beside me, Miu stared at Khepri in astonishment. "You want us to go into the storeroom?"

"Yes," Khepri said. "As fast as you can."

"The storeroom with two angry crocodiles in it?" I double-checked.

"Yes. Hurry, or it will be too late!"

"SOBEK JUNIOR!" King Sobek roared from inside the shed. And then: "WHO IS THIS BOY?"

I bolted for the storeroom.

The king and queen filled the room so completely that there was hardly any room for me amid the wreckage. But when I jumped onto a broken shelf, I saw some crunched-open feed bins at the back. Inside were three prisoners tied with rope. One was a baby crocodile. The second was a lion cub, fast asleep. The third was . . .

"Dedi!" I exclaimed, racing to his side. Bound and gagged, he couldn't speak, but his eyes brightened with hope. When he glanced back at the crocodile king and queen, the hope gave way to fear.

When I saw how the crocodiles were

looking at Dedi, I was afraid, too. Were they about to attack?

I jumped in front of Dedi and started talking fast.

"See?" I said to the crocodiles. "What did we tell you? Here is your baby, safe and sound. And our prince is with him. He was trying to save your prince, you see—"

"HE'S TIED UP!" the crocodile queen wailed. "MY BABY IS TIED UP!"

"DID THE BOY DO THAT?" King Sobek roared.

"Of course he didn't," I said. "He wouldn't. He's a very nice boy. I mean, sometimes he gets up to mischief, but that's how kids are, you know. And we love them anyway."

"HE'LL PAY FOR THIS," King Sobek said grimly.

"I'm telling you he didn't do it," I said, but he wasn't interested in me anymore, and neither was his wife. They were staring at Dedi, and they were gnashing their teeth.

I started to feel desperate. How could I keep them from attacking Dedi? "Look, I can free your baby, if that's what you want," I told the crocodiles. "I'll chew the ropes off myself."

The queen stopped gnashing. "YOU WILL?"

"HE'S JUST DISTRACTING US," King Sobek told her. "HE'LL TAKE ALL DAY."

"Not if I help." Miu leaped down beside me.

"I'll help, too," Khepri offered, hopping down from my head. "We'll be fast."

I have to admit, I never expected to find myself chewing away at a baby crocodile's ropes, but you do what you have to do, especially when the crocodile's angry parents are at your back.

Luckily, Sobek Junior had been rubbing at the ropes, shimmying against a rough spot inside the bin. We had him free in a jiffy.

He was such a young baby that his voice wasn't much more than a squeak. "Mommy! Daddy! You found me!"

"MY DARLING!" his mother sobbed. "COME HERE!"

She lowered her blunt snout to him, and he raced up to her back.

I joined Miu and Khepri in attacking Dedi's ropes. Like Sobek Junior, he'd been fraying them himself, and they quickly started to give way.

As the ropes fell off, Dedi reached for me, his arms shaking. "Ra."

Miu started in on the ropes around the lion cub. "I think maybe they drugged this one."

With a weak hand, Dedi unlatched the lid of a nearby basket. Two ibis hatchlings blinked up at us.

"THAT BOY," King Sobek roared to his son. "DID HE HURT YOU?"

"He *helped* me, Daddy," Sobek Junior piped cheerfully. "He was bringing me back to the river. Only we got caught."

"WHO CAUGHT YOU?" King Sobek demanded. "I'LL TEAR HIS GUTS OUT."

"NO." His wife was already backing out of the storeroom. "WE HAVE OUR BABY, AND I DON'T WANT ANY MORE TROUBLE. WE'RE GOING HOME."

King Sobek rumbled after her. "ALL RIGHT, WE'LL TAKE HIM HOME. BUT SOMEBODY IS GOING TO PAY FOR THIS. . . ."

As they headed for the dung pit, Dedi stumbled to the storehouse door. Miu and I went with him, Khepri riding on my head. We were just in time to see Sobek Junior wave his snout at us as he and his parents splashed down into the pit.

Lurching as if he were in a nightmare, Dedi sank down and knelt on the floor. "Sorry, Ra. My feet—they're numb from the ropes."

"Uh-oh," Khepri said. "That's not so good."

As I nuzzled Dedi's hand, trying to encourage him, Miu said, "We need to get help."

"And we need to see that justice is done," Khepri added, "now that we know who kidnapped him."

"Do we know that?" Miu asked.

"Of course we do," Khepri said. "Right, Ra?"

"Er . . . right," I confirmed.

Before I could fish for specifics, a hoarse whisper came from behind us. "How did you get out, boy?"

Dedi's kidnapper had found us.

CHAPTER 25

Tripped Up

Hormin sniffled and trained his spear on Dedi.

"Hormin?" Miu stared the spear in shock. "I never suspected him."

I hadn't, either. But Khepri didn't seem surprised.

Still sniffling, Hormin took a step closer to Dedi. "I should have finished you off last night."

Dedi tried to rise and run, but his numb feet tripped him up. He collapsed near the dung pit.

"That's right." Hormin came up behind him, spear raised. "Into that dung pit, boy. Or I'll spear you through the heart and *then* throw you in."

"No!" The Keeper careened down the passageway that led from the palace. Winded, he stopped just short of the dung pit. "You can't do this, Hormin. We'll have to deal with the boy some other way."

My ears swiveled in shock. The Keeper was Hormin's partner in crime?

"That's what you said last night, and look what happened," Hormin snarled at the Keeper. "We're dealing with him now. If he escapes, the whole game is up."

"But you promised me there wouldn't be any killing," the Keeper whined.

"Don't be stupid." Hormin kept the spear trained on Dedi. "You and Qen, what a pair! Both of you wanting to profit without getting any blood on your hands. Well, I've taken care of Qen, and I'll take care of you, too, if I have to."

"Taken care of Qen?" the Keeper repeated, trembling. "Hormin, what did you do?"

"He stumbled into a crocodile's path." Hormin's long face was expressionless. "He was having second thoughts, and I couldn't have him running to Pharaoh, could I?"

The Keeper was shaking even more now. "N-n-no."

"We have to get rid of the boy," Hormin said. "Don't you see? It's the only answer. He overheard everything we said. He'll go straight to his father, and then it's all over for us."

Dedi raised his head defiantly. "If you kill me, you'll just make things worse for yourselves when you're caught. And they're already bad enough."

For a moment, he sounded exactly like his father.

But then Hormin advanced with the spear, and Dedi became a twelve-year-old boy again, gulping and pulling back, back, back . . .

"Time to attack!" I cried.

Claws out, Miu and I darted at Hormin's kneecaps. Khepri leaped for his loincloth.

"Stupid cats!" Keeping the spear pointed at Dedi, Hormin kicked at us. Miu and I went spinning, and so did Khepri.

As we landed, stunned, Kiya came charging out of the zoo. "Don't you dare touch my brother!" she shouted at Hormin.

Unfortunately, she tripped over me, then tumbled into Dedi. Tangled together, we teetered on the edge of the dung pit.

"Guess what? You're going to have a little bath." A strange smile split Hormin's long face as he brought the spear closer. "A dung bath!"

"Never!" Miu rushed toward Hormin, but when he kicked at her again, she veered toward the zoo.

Miu was abandoning us? I couldn't believe it.

At least Khepri was still determined to help. Scrabbling to his feet, he crawled toward Hormin. But like most beetles, he was painfully slow.

"We're going to fall!" Kiya wailed.

Below us, the dung-water gurgled. I doubted even Khepri would want to end up there—not when it led straight to the Nile, and a kingdom of angry crocodiles.

The Keeper picked up a dung-mottled shovel.

"Khepri, stop him! He's going to finish us off!" I moaned.

But Khepri was too far away.

WHAM!

The Keeper's shovel hit Hormin's spear. With a clang, the spear fell to the ground. The Keeper kicked it into the dung pit.

Kiya, Dedi, and I rolled back from the edge and started scrambling away.

"What are you doing?" Hormin screamed at the Keeper. "We almost had them!"

"Some things aren't worth it," the Keeper told him. "Not even for an elephant."

"I'll kill you all," Hormin raged. "You and the kids and those stupid cats."

For a moment, it looked as though he might be strong enough to do it. But as he grabbed the shovel from the Keeper, a gabble of furious noise washed over us.

"The gate!" Khepri shouted. "Kiya forgot to close it. And maybe she opened some cages, too. And Miu . . ."

The rest of his words were drowned out by wild growling and howling and squawking and screeching. The zoo was on the move.

The lioness was the first out of the gate. Snarling, she drove Hormin to the edge of the dung pit. Behind her, the ibis and the monkeys went for the Keeper, who ran screaming into the storeroom. More animals followed, some of them looking dazed by their newfound freedom.

Last came Taweret the hippo—with Miu riding on her back. "Someone really was stealing the babies?" Taweret bellowed. "Take that, you lousy kidnapper!" Lowering her massive muzzle, she charged straight at Hormin.

Hormin lost his head. Rocking back on his heels, he dived into the dung pit.

Splash. Glop. Gloop. The dung-water closed over his head.

Everyone, even the monkeys, went silent as we waited for Hormin to rise up again. But all we heard was a faint crunch—and a *thump, thump, thump.*

Khepri said quietly, "Well, he made a mistake there."

"He certainly did," I agreed.

Crocodile justice is swift and harsh.

The lioness glared at Dedi and Kiya. "What about them? Are they guilty, too?"

"Of course not." Miu leaped down from Taweret to guard them. "Kiya's the one who opened your cages. And Dedi tried to rescue the baby crocodile."

"Oh, right." The lioness looked a little disappointed.

"What do we do now?" Taweret wondered.

"Escape," Miu suggested. "If you want to, that is. I think I hear people coming—and they might have spears. So now's the time."

I have never seen animals move so fast. (And that includes me when I'm snatching a snack from the banquet table.) Within a minute, the lion had three of her cubs on her back. Grabbing the sleepy one with her mouth, she vaulted through a high window and over the moat.

"Hold on to my feathers, my dears," the ibis told her hatchlings as she flapped through the window. The monkeys were practically flying as they left, too. Crocodiles snapped at them in vain as they scampered over debris that had flooded into the moat.

Taweret watched them go. "Actually, I think I might stay. I never did like having to share my pond with crocodiles."

As she wandered back to her mud pond,

I heard familiar footsteps pounding toward us. Dedi and Kiya couldn't hear them yet—they don't have cats' ears—but I jumped up and ran into the passageway.

"Ra!" Spear in hand, Pharaoh looked as frantic as I'd ever seen him. "Ra, where are my children?"

With a triumphant meow, I led him to Dedi and Kiya.

CHAPTER 26

The Surprise

"Kiya! Dedi!" Pharaoh cast down his spear and swept them up in his arms. Behind them, Pharaoh's guards fanned out.

Within moments, Kiya was telling Pharaoh and Dedi about her adventures. "I hid in a crate. And then I went looking for Dedi. Only Turo caught me."

"He hurt you?" Pharaoh clenched his fists.

Kiya flattened his fists, as if it were a game. "Oh, no. He was very nice to me. He even gave me a snack. But he told me I had to stay hidden. He was worried that someone had kidnapped Dedi—and they might try to kidnap me. But I didn't want to stay hidden. I wanted to find Dedi. So I did."

By the time she finished her story, Pharaoh was holding both children so tight that they were starting to squirm. When he finally released them, he traced their faces with his fingertips.

"You're safe," he murmured again and again. "You're alive. You're safe."

After all we'd been through, I could barely believe it myself. I nuzzled the children's hands, just to be sure it wasn't a dream.

"Ra-baby!" Kiya hauled me up from the floor. "Daddy, Ra saved us from going over into the pit. He was a hero!"

She was clutching me too hard around the middle, but for once I didn't care.

Pharaoh lifted me into his arms and stroked under my chin, my favorite spot. "I should have known you would find a way to keep them safe, Ra the Mighty. Even Bastet herself could not have done better."

I purred and purred and purred. Pharaoh's praise was sweet—and it was even sweeter to know I deserved it. I was Pharaoh's Cat, Lord of the Powerful Paw, and I had done my duty. I had found Dedi. I had protected Kiya. And . . .

My gaze fell on Miu, sitting quietly a few feet away, with Khepri beside her.

Yes, I had done my duty. But I hadn't done it alone. With a loud meow, I jumped down from Pharaoh's arms and led him over to Miu and Khepri.

"That's the other cat, Daddy!" Kiya hopped over to stroke Miu. "She helped, too. And the beetle. They were all there, protecting us."

Pharaoh smiled. "Well, then, they have my thanks, too."

You'd think it would be hard, having to share my glory. But it turned out to be as easy as watching the sun rise. And when I looked at my friends, I felt a warm, sunshiny glow inside me. Sometimes in life you get lucky, and you get more than one family. Miu and Khepri, I realized, were part of mine.

Beside us, Dedi started telling his side of the story to Pharaoh.

"Wow." Khepri gazed up at me, dazzled. "Did you hear that, Ra? Pharaoh *thanked* me."

"He thanked us both," said Miu, sounding pleased. "He's a good man."

"You deserve it," I said. "I couldn't have done it without you."

"No, you couldn't," Khepri agreed cheerfully. "But it was you who finally cracked the case, Ra."

"Oh, yeah," I mumbled. "That's right. I did, didn't I?"

"How did you figure it out?" Miu asked me.

"Well, er . . . it was easy, you see . . . I . . . er . . ." I floundered. How *had* I worked it out? I couldn't quite remember.

"You don't need to be so modest, Ra." Khepri turned to Miu. "Ra asked the vital question. *What use is a lion cub to anyone?*"

"Yes, that's what I said," I confirmed. Though, to be honest, I didn't understand why it mattered so much.

"The answer, of course, is that a lion cub is worth quite a lot," Khepri said. "As Ra mentioned when we arrived, zoos are fashionable right now. Lots of rich people want to buy unusual animals like ibises and lions and crocodiles. And that's why baby animals were disappearing from Lady Satiah's zoo. Hormin, Qen, and the Keeper were smuggling them out and secretly selling them. But they were very sneaky about it. Even the animals didn't realize what was happening."

"The ibis blamed the lion cubs for eating her hatchlings," I remembered.

"And when the lioness said her cub had

been stolen," Miu recalled, "we didn't take her seriously because we thought he was sick."

"I figured the Keeper had to be involved if animals were disappearing," Khepri said. "It couldn't be done without him. But I guessed he had help. It's no easy thing to sneak a lion cub out of a palace."

"How did you work out it was Hormin and Qen?" Miu wanted to know.

"I remembered how handy they were with the nets when they captured the lion cub in the banqueting hall," Khepri said. "The Keeper turned to them again when he wanted to catch another crocodile. No one else except the Keeper seemed to be so handy with animals—especially with trapping them.

"Plus, they were the ones who guarded the palace at night," Khepri went on. "And night would be the best time to move the animals, without anyone hearing growls or squawks. They could even creep out to the landing and get access to the river."

I had to hand it to him. It all made sense.

"I expect they were working with someone on the outside," Khepri mused. "Maybe the animals were picked up by boat."

"And the storeroom was the holding bay for the animals that were going to be shipped out?" Miu guessed.

"Yes," Khepri said. "And remember what Taweret the hippo told us? She overheard Dedi say that he needed a basket to carry the crocodile. And baskets are kept in—"

"The storeroom!" I said triumphantly.

"So that's how Dedi got involved," Miu said. "He stumbled right into the headquarters of the whole operation."

"Yes," Khepri said. "And if they had places to store young animals awaiting shipment, I figured they probably had places to stow a young boy."

"And you were right." Miu curled her tail fondly around him.

"It was a smooth operation," Khepri said. "They hid Dedi and the crocodile, and then one of the watchmen made footprints outside and set a boat loose to make it look like Dedi had run away."

"We thought someone had kidnapped Dedi because they didn't want him to be the crown prince," Miu said. "We missed the real motive."

"But it's hard to fool Pharaoh's Cat," I said proudly. "I asked the right question."

"You did." Khepri tapped my forepaw. "In the end."

"We saved Dedi," Miu said with satisfaction. "And Kiya. And we helped the whole zoo."

"We did," I agreed. Really, we'd outdone ourselves this time.

"I just have one question," Miu said to Khepri. "Lady Satiah was definitely up to something, even if it wasn't kidnapping Dedi. We still don't know—"

"Shhh!" Khepri warned. "Here she comes."

Behind us, Lady Satiah was approaching. Pharaoh and the children fell silent. The only sound was the Keeper, blubbering in the storeroom wreckage, with Pharaoh's guards around him.

"Keeper, is that you?" Frowning, Lady Satiah hurried toward him.

Catching sight of Pharaoh, she stopped and sank into a deep curtsy. "O Most Gracious Ruler of Rulers, Exalted Husband of

Husbands, your son Ahmose awaits you with his tutor in the . . ." She broke off as she took in the two children behind him. "Dedi? Kiya? You're here?" She glared at them both. "What kind of tricks have you been playing? You should be ashamed—"

"There was no trick," Pharaoh said gravely, holding Dedi and Kiya close. "And they are not the ones who should be ashamed. They were in danger, here in your house."

"In danger? Nonsense!" Lady Satiah flounced up from her curtsy, her wig askew. "I don't know what they've been telling you, but it isn't true. I told you in my message that you shouldn't worry, and I was right. They were fine. See? Here they are."

"Only because they were resourceful," Pharaoh said.

"And because of Ra and his friends," Kiya reminded him.

"Yes," Pharaoh agreed. To Lady Satiah, he said, "I had a warning that something was wrong here, so I came to find my children."

"A *warning*?" Lady Satiah tensed. "What do you mean?"

"Yesterday morning, my guards caught

a dangerous criminal in Thebes," Pharaoh told her. "I remained there to be certain they caught his accomplices, too."

"So that's why Pharaoh stayed in Thebes!" Khepri whispered.

"And why he sent the children away," Miu murmured.

Pharaoh went on, "The leader confessed that his network included men in your household, Lady Satiah. I set out immediately. We were halfway here when your messenger reached me. But I would have gone faster still, had I known you had a murderer on the loose."

"A murderer?" Lady Satiah sounded faint. "It was Yaba, wasn't it? She's a spy. An assassin. That's why I locked her up—"

"You did *what*?" Pharaoh thundered. "Release her at once!"

"But she—"

"Lady Yaba had nothing to do with this." Pharaoh's voice was as hard and sharp as his spear. "It was your Keeper and your watchmen who kidnapped my son. And Hormin tried to kill both Kiya and Dedi."

"The watchmen and the Keeper were part

of a smuggling ring," Dedi explained. "They were selling baby animals from your zoo."

"What?" Under her painted face, Lady Satiah suddenly looked sick. "Is this true?"

"Yes," Dedi told her. "I went into the storeroom to get a basket for the crocodile, but then Hormin, Qen, and the Keeper came in, and I had to hide. They talked about selling some ibis hatchlings and maybe the baby crocodile and a lion cub, too. I tried to sneak away, but they saw me, and Hormin hit me. Later, he tried to kill me."

"I'm sorry!" the Keeper wailed as Pharaoh's guards closed in on him. "I didn't mean for anyone to get hurt. I wanted the babies to go to good homes, with owners who love them. And Hormin said I could make enough to buy my own elephant, too. But nobody was supposed to get killed." He started sobbing again. "I'm really, truly sorry."

"Sorry?" Lady Satiah glared at him through her kohl-rimmed eyes. "You'll be more than sorry when I'm through with you, Keeper. And Hormin and Qen will be, too. You've completely spoiled my surprise."

Pharaoh stared at her in disbelief. "Is that your only concern? That some surprise has been spoiled?"

Lady Satiah didn't seem to notice anything was wrong. "The surprise was for you."

Pharaoh shook his head. "I have had enough surprises today."

"But this is a wonderful one," Lady Satiah pleaded. "No other wife has ever given you so royal a gift. You must accept it!"

Pharaoh looked at her, mystified.

Lady Satiah waved grandly at the gate. "Here it is before you, O Ruler of Rulers! Your very own zoo!"

"That's the surprise?" I muttered to Khepri and Miu.

"It is to Pharaoh," Miu said.

"But maybe not quite the way she meant it to be," Khepri added.

"They're all yours," Lady Satiah told Pharaoh. "The lions, the ibises, the monkeys, even the hippo. I've collected an entire zoo, all for you."

Pharaoh looked at Lady Satiah blankly. "But I don't want a zoo."

"Of course you want a zoo," Lady Satiah said frantically. "Everyone does."

"Not me," Pharaoh said. "I travel too much." He smiled down at me. "Besides, I have a cat."

"Anyway," Kiya told Lady Satiah, "your zoo is gone."

"Don't be ridiculous." Lady Satiah stalked to the gate. "My zoo is—"

She caught sight of the empty cages.

"*Gone!*" she wailed.

CHAPTER 27

The Royal Babysitter

The next morning, as we gathered in the great hall, Hoop showed up again. It took a while to catch him up on everything.

"So that was Lady Satiah's big plan?" Hoop shrieked with laughter. "She talked the General into helping her fund a zoo so they could give it to Pharaoh? And they thought he'd be so thrilled that he'd give them whatever they wanted? Oop-oop. Of all the half-baked ideas!"

"To be fair, you have to remember that she doesn't see much of Pharaoh," Miu said. "She didn't know he doesn't like zoos. Lots of rich people do."

"Fools!" Hoop dismissed them. "Why

232

keep animals in cages? Everyone knows it's better when you can fly around and catch your own bugs."

Khepri slid down to my belly.

"Not you, you little dung-eater!" Hoop chortled. "Oop-oop. Anyway, I've already had my breakfast."

"So have I," I said as Khepri peeked out from my belly fur. "Don't poke too hard there, Khepri. I'm on the full side."

Since we'd closed the case, I'd pretty much been eating nonstop. Pharaoh had insisted that every delicacy be offered to me. I had to hand it to the cooks. Stewed oxtail, braised antelope, cinnamon-glazed duck—everything was excellent. But best of all was the expression on Lady Satiah's face as I sampled my treats from her very own plates.

She was still giving me the evil eye even now. That is, when she wasn't trying to give Ahmose his instructions.

"Remember your manners," she said, smoothing his hair. "Write to me every day. And don't let your tunic sashes drag on the floor."

"Don't worry, my lady," Turo said. "I'll look after him."

"Ahmose is going away?" Hoop flicked his crown feathers in amazement. "Where to?"

"He's going with us," I told him.

"So her plan worked!" Hoop shrieked. "Pharaoh adores her boy. She got what she wanted!"

"Not quite," Khepri said from the safety of my belly. "Lady Satiah is in disgrace. Pharaoh is removing Ahmose from her influence for a while and having him educated with Dedi. Turo's coming, too, and he's getting a promotion. Pharaoh says he's earned it since he did his best to protect Kiya."

"Lady Satiah will stay here with the General," Miu added. "Pharaoh says they'll both be supervised, and they'll have their travel curtailed for a while."

"She'll need to replace her Steward and Painter," Hoop said. "I saw them grab a boat and head down the Nile last night, as fast as the river could carry them. Oop-oop!"

"Yes," Miu said, "but they left Dedi's jewelry behind. I guess they got scared when Pharaoh arrived and Dedi turned up alive. Stealing from Pharaoh's family is treason."

"And Qen?" Hoop dipped his head feathers. "I heard he survived the crocodiles, no thanks to Hormin."

"Qen's bandaged up now," Khepri said, "and he'll go on trial with the rest of the smuggling gang. I guess he's discovered there are worse things than being a watchman."

"What about Yaba?" Hoop wanted to know.

"She and Pharaoh have gotten to know each other a little better," I said. "When Pharaoh realized how homesick she was, he offered to send her back, but she says her father would only marry her to someone else. She asked instead for a home of her own, far away from Lady Satiah, and he's granting her that."

"She'll take the gazelle with her, too," Miu said. "The one she sings to. It has a short leg and can't survive in the wild."

"Yaba said she'd take Taweret, too," Khepri put in. "And Taweret's baby, when it's born. And the Keeper is going with them."

"The Keeper?" Hoop fluttered his wings in surprise. "But he stole all those baby animals."

"Yes, he did," Miu said. "But he really did believe he was giving them a good home, and he stopped Hormin from hurting Dedi and Kiya. So Pharaoh has decided to let him off lightly. He has to give his profits back, and he owes a big fine, but he can go with Yaba. She says that one day she might even let him have an elephant—but only if it's one that can't live in the wild."

"Oop-oop!" Hoop flew up. "Sounds like Pharaoh's calling you guys. Toodle-oop-oop!"

It was time to go. Quicker than I would have thought possible, we were settled on the deck of Pharaoh's royal barge, getting ready to head home.

"I need to speak with the captain," Pharaoh said to the children. "But Ra the Mighty will look after you."

"And so will his friends," Miu added.

"You bet!" Khepri said. "The Great Detectives are great at looking after things."

"Thanks, guys." I stretched out in the

sun. "How about we *look* for a snack *after* I have a nap?"

But then Kiya cornered me.

Oh, no, I thought. *Dress-up time.*

"Ra-baby," Kiya cooed. "I know how much you love dress-up—"

Oh, no, I don't.

"—but I've decided it's kind of boring," Kiya went on.

Well, that was great news. I nuzzled her hand to show how pleased I was.

"I've got a great new game for us instead." Kiya rose to her feet. "It's called *crocodile!*"

She charged at me, arms snapping together like jaws.

"You know, I think I'd rather play dress-up!" I yowled to Miu and Khepri.

But when they laughed and joined in the game, I did, too. Family is family, after all. And I was glad to have mine.

I was Ra the Mighty, Pharaoh's Cat, Lord of the Powerful Paw. And if that meant I was also Ra the Royal Babysitter, that was just fine by me.

Ra's Glossary
of Names

Ahmose (*ah*-mose): Son of Pharaoh and Lady Satiah. A nice kid who wants a pet. (A pet crocodile, that is.)

Dedi (*ded*-ee): The crown prince, Pharaoh's number one son and heir. More sensible than his sister, but not to be trusted with a lizard.

Hormin (*hoar*-meen): A tall, sniffly watchman. Handy with a net.

Khepri (*kep-ree):* Insect investigator. My scarab beetle buddy and fellow Great Detective. Definitely not a snack.

Kiya (*kee*-yah): Pharaoh's daredevil younger daughter. Mischief-maker. Keeper of the costumes.

Nekhbet (*nek*-bet): A birdbrain who pals around with crocodiles. Not a cultured vulture.

Miu *(mew):* Another Great Detective. Kitchen cat and confronter of crocodiles.

Qen *(ken):* A short, red-nosed watchman who's ready for a break.

Ramses Dedumose (*rahm*-sees *ded*-oo-mose): see Dedi

Satiah (sah-*tee*-ah): Ahmose's mother. A woman with a plan . . . and a zoo.

Sobek (*so*-bek): A crocodile-headed god—and also a scaly king and his heir (Sobek Junior). Watch out for the teeth!

Taweret (*tah*-oo-ret): Earth mother and happy hippo. Always up for a mud bath.

Turo (*too*-row): Ahmose's cousin and curly-headed tutor. Stronger than he looks.

Wegaf (wey-*gaff*): Lady Satiah's brother. A general with bad dreams.

Yaba (*yah*-bah): One of Pharaoh's wives. A princess without power, and a sleepwalker with a secret.

Author's Note

Have you ever seen the crocodile god Sobek? I have . . .

. . . well, a statue of him, anyway. He guards an ancient Egyptian temple in one of my favorite museums. His huge head sits on a plinth, and he has a sleek wig and fearsome teeth. He's impossible to ignore. Every time I see him, I can almost hear him asking, "When are you going to write about crocodiles?"

Now that I have, I hope he's pleased.

As the statue indicates, ancient Egyptians were fascinated with crocodiles. No wonder, because they are astonishing animals. Closely related to their dinosaur-era ancestors, they look a lot like them, too. Their bite is stronger than that of any other creature, and they can stay underwater for hours, lying in wait for their prey. Their blood is special as well, with factors in it that help them heal quickly.

Ancient Egyptians were aware of two types of

crocodile: the Nile crocodile (*Crocodylus niloticus*) and the West African crocodile (*Crocodylus suchus*). Both were associated with Sobek, a complicated deity who represented fertility, power, protection, aggression, and Pharaoh.

Egyptian priests tended to use West African crocodiles in their ceremonies, probably because they are smaller and less ferocious than Nile crocodiles. I decided, however, to put Nile crocodiles in the waters by Lady Satiah's palace. They can be upwards of fifteen feet long and weigh over four hundred pounds, and they consider humans fair game. In modern times, they were hunted almost to extinction, but they have since made a comeback. So if you visit the Nile, watch out for them!

The Nile was the great highway of ancient Egypt, but we still have a lot to learn about the vessels that traveled it. The earliest Egyptian boats were made with bundles of reeds. The reeds held a lot of air inside them, so they were good at floating. By Ra's time, many royal boats were built with wood, including cedar of Lebanon. These vessels could be both large and fancy, with sails, steering oars, and cabins on deck for important passengers.

Most pharaohs spent plenty of time traveling up and down the Nile. They needed to keep an eye on various parts of their kingdom, and they had to attend important religious festivals in different cities. They tended to move from palace to palace throughout the year.

Pharaohs also tended to marry more than one wife, and some of these marriages were made for diplomatic reasons. Pharaoh's Great Wife—the chief wife—usually lived with him, but his other wives were sometimes removed to another palace, along with their children. Some of those wives must have felt homesick and isolated, like Lady Yaba.

A pharaoh had the power to decide whom he named as his heir, so someone like Lady Satiah could hope that her own son might impress him and eventually ascend to the throne. There were other ways for a wife to gain power, too. Khepri's story about the royal wife who led a plot against the pharaoh is true, as far as we can tell. The wife's name was Tiye, the pharaoh's name was Ramses III—and he really did end up dead.

A few more true details: Royal servants did indeed have fancy job titles like Painter of Her Mouth. Twenty Squares really was the name of a favorite game in ancient Egypt. And Pharaoh and his court really did regard fish as taboo.

We also know that ancient Egyptians associated cats with the goddess Bastet, who was said to protect women and children. Cats were probably the most popular pet in ancient Egypt. Some nobles preferred more exotic animals, such as lions, monkeys, baboons, antelope, leopards, and crocodiles. These animals were expensive to obtain and to keep, and their cost and rarity made them status symbols.

Scholars argue about whether ancient Egyptians kept actual zoos, but there's some compelling evidence that they did, and that a hippo like Taweret might end up in one. Sadly, there's also evidence that many of the animals were not treated well.

I don't think anyone in Egypt ever tried to put a hoopoe

in a zoo, but they are amazing birds. Their head feathers make them look like glamorous punk-rock stars. Their nickname is the butterfly bird, and they like to nest in cliffs and walls. They consider dung beetles delicious, and they do indeed say "Oop-oop!"

Acknowledgments

Mighty thanks to all my partners in crime, including Sarah Horne, whose marvelous illustrations bring Ra and his friends to life; Sally Morgridge, Derek Stordahl, Mary Cash, Terry Borzumato-Greenberg, Kevin Jones, Nicole Benevento, Lex Higbee, Emily Mannon, Hannah Finne, Eryn Levine, Amy Toth, and the other wonderful people at Holiday House, who bring Ra and his friends to readers; Barbara Perris, whose stellar copyediting spruces Ra up; Sara Crowe, Larissa Helena, Ashley Valentine, Cameron Chase, and rest of the fabulous Pippins, who are enthusiastic about all things Ra; and Tracy Abell and Kit Sturtevant, two fantastic writers who gave me helpful comments on an early draft of this book.

I'm also grateful to my parents, who let me have lots of books and kittens when I was small; to Rebecca Sokolovsky and her family, who cheer for Ra and make my New York travels more fun; to the Ashmolean in Oxford, where Sobek guards the Ancient Egypt galleries; and to Crocodiles of the World in Brize Norton, England, where I researched crocodiles up close (and saw how high they can jump!). I also want to thank all the teachers, librarians, booksellers, bloggers, friends, and fans who have shared their love for the Great Detectives. Your posts, emails, photos, letters, tweets, video clips, and drawings are a delight.

Finally, my loving thanks to my husband and daughter—Ra's number one fans, readers, and plot consultants, who always make sure that Ra and his scribe get enough snacks and naps!